FREE FALL

FREE FALL

ELIZABETH BARRETT

HarperCollins*Publishers*

Library of Congress Cataloging-in-Publication Data
Barrett, Elizabeth
Free Fall / by Elizabeth Barrett.
p. cm.
Summary: Spending the summer with her grandmother while her parents try to
sort out their troubled marriage, seventeen-year-old Ginnie gropes with unex-
pected romance, curiosity about sex, and the problems of growing up.
ISBN 0-06-024465-8. — ISBN 0-06-024466-6 (lib. bdg.)
[1. Family problems—Fiction. 2. Grandmothers—Fiction. 3. Sexual ethics—
Fiction.] I. Title.
PZ7.B2748Fr 1994   93-44160
[Fic]—dc20   CIP
                                                                       AC

Typography by Carole Goodman
1   2   3   4   5   6   7   8   9   10

First Edition

With thanks to my mother, Margaret, and Sue,
and to my fellow writers at the
Molasses Pond Writers Conference, 1988.

And in memory of Margaret Smith Barron.

O N E

have no suitcases of my own, except a green overnight
bag Grandma and Grandpa gave me when I was ten.
Small and flimsy, it fits easily into the trunk of Dad's
Chevy. The big, boxy suitcase Mom loaned me, with its
faded University of Pittsburgh sticker melded onto it,
jams into a corner of the trunk, behind two boxes filled
with books and tapes, shoes and shorts and T-shirts. Dad
has only one small bag himself. He's taking me to Pittsburgh, staying at Grandma's for one night, then turning
back to Philadelphia. I'm staying all summer.

On the way out he lets me drive for thirty minutes, not
through the mountains but on the flat stretch around
Harrisburg. I carefully hold the speedometer at fifty-five,
signaling before I pull into the left lane to pass a car,
singing along with the radio until I remember Dad and

that he might think I'm not paying enough attention to the road. I'm in control for thirty minutes, pretending he isn't there and the new blue Chevy is small, sporty, and red; that I am not seventeen but twenty-three, my hair long and glossy black instead of summer-short and just dark brown; that I am not skinny but elegantly lean, like a model, languid and enigmatic, not gawky and anxious to please. Pretending I got off at Carlisle and took Route 81 to Maryland, Virginia, wherever, wandering into a new and marvelous life, like Lauren Bacall in *To Have and Have Not*.

The fantasy's not new. I've never wanted to be what I am. When I was nine, I wanted to be a horse. Actually, I wanted to own a horse, but my parents told me I couldn't. But they took me riding sometimes, and that one time, when I was nine and we were driving away from the stables, I started crying.

"I want to be a horse!" I said. I truly did. I'd only be happy as a horse, galloping around fields, shaking my mane and flicking my tail, snorting and whinnying and always looking handsome. Not a girl.

My older brother, Tom, tried to help. He had my beach ball, the pink one with the specks of bright color inside that I lost at the Jersey shore the next summer, and he pretended it was magic. He twirled it around and said, "Now you're a horse."

The make-believe didn't work, and I cried all the way home.

Then when I was thirteen I wanted to be a boy. I knew I didn't have any choice, but the girls in my classes were such giggling, primping prisses, and I much preferred the way the boys laughed, and how they didn't care when teachers reprimanded them. I wore baggy shirts that hid my breasts, and when I crossed my legs I rested my ankle on my knee, the way boys did, and never thigh on thigh, the way girls did. Not, of course, that it made any difference.

Now I'm seventeen, and I still don't want to be myself.

Dad takes over the driving, whipping us through the six tunnels between Carlisle and Pittsburgh, while I sit rigidly, willing no one to hit us. I loved the tunnels when I was a child. They were two-way then, and dark, the openings arched and the walls rough concrete. The openings are rectangular now; inside, the two lanes are one-way, and the sun-bright lights gleam off pale, glossy tiles.

But the lanes are too narrow, the cars' speed exaggerated by the hard, bright walls. The thick yellow line is no protection from a car that might veer in front of us and send us crashing into those walls. I stare at the small square of light, the distant exit, our escape. We burst from the fluorescent-lit tunnel into the sunshine. I rest against the seat. Cheated death again.

The driveway to Grandma's house, in a western suburb of Pittsburgh, is narrow. Thorny bushes line it and scrape gently along the sides of the car. As Dad stops in front of the garage, the back door opens and Grandma appears on the porch. She waits there, her plump body squeezed into violet linen, not speaking or even waving as I follow the slate stepping-stones from the drive to the porch. She seems to need to evaluate me before greeting me, to see what changes I've sustained. I step up onto the porch, and she finally smiles and holds her arms open for a hug.

Grandma is short, more than half a foot shorter than me, and age and a hunched and twisted back have stooped her even lower. Her hair is blond and curled, the gray rinsed out of it, and her eyes are as wide and blue as the morning glories that edge her garden. Our hug is strong but quick. Though my arms are long enough to encircle her firm body, I hold myself away. We are not a family that hugs.

"Hello, hello!" she cries, cupping my face in her hands so she can kiss me.

"Hello!" Dad calls from the car. He is already unloading the trunk. "How are you, Mother?"

"Oh . . ." She laughs, a girlish trickle of sound that could mean anything. "I'm just fine, Richard. Would you like something cold to drink?"

"Love it. Ginnie, come help me unload."

I slip down off the porch, not bothering with the stepping-stones as I walk back to the car. Dissatisfaction at having arrived adds iron weights to my arms and legs. I never like the end of trips. Newton's law that a body in motion tends to want to stay in motion applies to me. When traveling, I want the car to keep on going, loving the effortless whir of the tires, the movielike view of farms and towns and strip mines, the road that curves and dips and rises unendingly. A destination is never as good as the anticipation, and the freedom of traveling is squashed by greetings and unpacking and finding something to do. Traveling is doing, complete in itself.

4

We have the car unloaded and everything inside in three trips. Stately and large, Grandma's house is different from every other one on the street. Where we live, my parents, Tom, and I, the brick houses are all alike. The only differences are garage doors and the color of the shutters. Our living room and dining room together are barely larger than Grandma's living room alone, and we certainly don't have a fireplace.

Upstairs are three bedrooms—my grandmother's, the guest room, and my mother's. My mother's is small and perfect, painted cream and always neat. There are only three pieces of furniture—a high, firm spool bed, an armless chair with a cane seat, and a vanity table. The legs of the vanity are hidden behind filmy white fabric, fastened to arms that swing out to reveal one tiny drawer. Grandma always keeps lacy handkerchiefs in the drawer.

Dad and I carry my suitcases and boxes upstairs and leave them on the floor of the bedroom. They fill nearly all the space between the closet and the vanity, and I wonder how Mom survived in such a little room.

I will stay in that room this summer. I'll climb into the high bed every night. I'll hang my clothes in the closet, where Grandma keeps her out-of-season dresses; stack my books on the floor; and clutter the vanity with my brush and comb and hair barrettes, my deodorant and bits of jewelry and the perfume I bought at the drugstore.

My parents have gotten rid of me again.

T W O

Mom told me on a Sunday, the sleepy, lazy mid-May Sunday after the junior prom. I had laid my soft blue-and-white gown across the spare bed in my room, partly to check for rips and stains but mostly to stroke the satin, shivering at the memory of my boyfriend's hands on my hips as we slow-danced. I had made the gown, and generously complimented myself on a fine job. Fitted to the waist, with an off-the-shoulder neckline and a swirling skirt, the dress, in my opinion, looked better lying on the bed than it did on me. But nothing looked right on my lanky, bony body.

I had found some dirt ground into the hem—I'd probably stepped on it while dancing—when Mom knocked on the door.

"Come in," I called.

She did, and smiled when she saw the gown. "Any damage?"

I shrugged, not looking up. "Just this."

She glanced at the hem. "Doesn't look too bad. Why don't you put it on the chair in my bedroom? I'll take it to the cleaners tomorrow."

"Okay." I gathered the gown to myself, turning to leave the room. She stood between me and the door, though, and didn't move. I had to look up, and for a moment we gazed at each other.

When I was little people said we looked alike, but not any longer. I'd grown to be three inches taller than she, and was thinner. Of course, she'd once been thinner, too, before she'd had two children. Even her face was heavier, the chin sagging just a bit, the cheeks plumping as if she'd recovered some baby fat. My cheeks had been plump, too, yet now the skin lay flat between sharp cheekbones and sharp jaw, emphasizing my prowlike nose.

People suggested, seeing Mom and me now, that I took after my father. But even his face had a rounder, softer quality, like my brother Tom's. Mom would say that I looked like my paternal grandmother, a woman I didn't remember. She died when I was three. A picture of her and my grandfather stood on my father's dresser, Grandpa Ryan looking just like Dad and smiling broadly; my grandmother posing awkwardly, a summer cotton dress dropping straight from her broad shoulders and pulled in at her waist, revealing that she—like me—had no curves between flat chest and flat hips. Her smile was as stiff as her posture, more a pursing of her lips, and one arm hung gracelessly on Grandpa's.

"I need to talk with you, Ginnie," Mom said as I folded the gown over my arm. She moved to sit on the spare bed, and I backed a few feet to my own bed.

"What is it?" I asked, sitting cross-legged, the gown covering my lap.

"It's about this summer."

"I'm not going back to camp."

"I know." She glanced out the window behind me. "I wasn't going to suggest that. I'm sorry it wasn't . . . I'm sorry you didn't have a good time there."

I turned my own gaze away, to the open door. Camp hadn't been so bad, except that I hadn't wanted to be there. It had been her idea. So I told her I'd had a lousy time.

"What I'd like you to consider," Mom went on after a minute, "is spending a few weeks out in Pittsburgh with Grandma."

I frowned. "Why?"

"Because she's lonely out there, now that Grandpa's gone. And she doesn't see much of you and Tom anymore. I think it would be good for both of you to spend more time together."

You've got to be joking, I thought. "What would I do in Pittsburgh?"

She shrugged. "What do you do here during the summer?"

"Mom, I do have friends here. And a boyfriend."

Mentioning Denny was risky. Neither of my parents liked him, and I'd just gotten over being grounded because he and I had stayed out past my curfew earlier that month.

"Some of your friends go away for the summer," she said, ignoring Denny. "And you know people in Pittsburgh."

"Who?"

"The Webers. The people who live across the street from Grandma."

I plucked at the dirty threads of the hem. If my radio hadn't been so far away, sitting on the windowsill at the head of my bed, I would have turned it on to end the conversation. None of our conversations were long these days.

She stayed for another minute, then stood. "I'm sure it would please your grandmother very much. And it would only be for a few weeks."

"I'll think about it."

She left, closing the door behind her, and I fell back on the bed. Pulling the gown up to my face, I could faintly smell my perfume and sweat. The combination was nauseating, and I pushed the gown away.

Pittsburgh. Why did she want me to go to Pittsburgh? When Tom and I were younger, we'd fly out to Pittsburgh alone and spend a week with Grandma and Grandpa. Neither of us had done that for years, though. Visits to Pittsburgh were usually just over a three-day weekend, and Grandma would spend Christmas, Easter, and part of the summer with us in Philadelphia. Pittsburgh? What would I do in Pittsburgh?

Of course, Mom had me there. What would I do in

Philadelphia? After my four weeks in camp last summer, I'd been bored and then depressed living at home. Mom wasn't there, having gone up to Maine for July and August, living in a small oceanfront cottage she'd rented with two college friends. It was just me and Dad, since Tom, once again, was working as a counselor at a canoeing camp on the Allagash River in Maine. Dad wasn't great company, at work all day and in front of the TV all night. Or out.

I could still smell the gown and rolled off the bed, carrying it with me. Let it stink up their bedroom. Out in the hall, I glided across the top of the stairs, listening.

They were in the living room. The television was on, a baseball game. From the voices, I placed Dad near the stairs in his black vinyl recliner, and Mom over by the door, either sitting on the couch or standing. She didn't seem to sit much these days.

"—she say?" Dad was asking.

"She doesn't want to go," Mom answered. "I expected that."

I heard a creaking of vinyl and rustling of paper, the eternal Sunday *New York Times*—which both my parents preferred over any local paper. "If she really doesn't want to go . . . "

"Richard. We've talked about this. It's the best thing for all of us."

I nearly charged down the stairs at that. I seriously doubted it was best for me, or that "best for me" came into their reasoning at all. I stomped loudly the rest of the way to their bedroom, just to let them know I'd heard. Not that either would be surprised, or even bother to scold me for eavesdropping. I'd been doing it for years, since I was six or so, starting right there at the top of the stairs.

It began when I'd woken up one night a few hours after I'd been put to bed and wanted my mother. She and Dad were in the living room with company, and I sat on the top step, too shy to go all the way down in my nightgown into the midst of those big, tall strangers. I didn't actually listen to what they were saying that night, but was intrigued by how my parents sounded, laughing together, my father's voice full and lively instead of workweary. They were different people, and every time they had company I was drawn back to the stairs, trying to learn who they were.

Whenever my mother saw me, my bare feet just visible from the living room, I would tell her I'd had a bad dream. That only worked a few times. Although I couldn't hear as well, I resigned myself to sitting in the hallway above the stairs, leaning my head down as far as I could. If I sensed someone starting for the stairs, I'd run into the bathroom and flush the toilet. I couldn't have been eavesdropping if I'd been in the bathroom.

What I heard then still didn't interest me, and I quickly forgot it. The wrongness and the implicit danger of eavesdropping fascinated me. I loved the way my heart beat rapidly and my stomach clenched as I stood poised in the hall, waiting to see which direction the footsteps in the living room would go.

Eventually I grew too big to lurk at the top of the stairs, but there were other conversations to listen to. Between my parents, my brother and my parents, my brother and his friends, phone calls. I still got caught, usually by my mother. Although she was not the yelling type, her normally strong voice would grow even louder with exasperation. She would vow that the next time she caught me, she'd punish me. She'd also remind me that eavesdroppers never hear anything good about themselves.

That last bit of wisdom I treated as a parent's normal attempt to manipulate her child's behavior with ridiculous warnings. By the time I was twelve, I was paying attention to what I heard, and only rarely caught the sound of my own name. Usually just my father asking, his voice lusterless as he turned on the television, "Did the kids behave today? How's Ginnie's cold?"

What did they think of me? Or did they think of me at all? Even when I rebelled against my middle-class suburban upbringing—wearing tight tops and jeans with holes and tears in them to school, my friends no longer the nice, polite girls I'd played with before, but the kids who hung out on the street corners and smoked in the school bathrooms—I didn't rate in the conversations I overheard between my parents. I concluded that either they were talking in the middle of the night, and on the phone when I was at school, or they weren't talking about me at all.

I should be grateful, I thought, as I tossed my prom dress onto the armchair in their bedroom, that they were talking about me now.

Mom didn't mention my going to Pittsburgh again for a while, and neither did I. We did speak to each other, briefly, flatly, every day, but I was practicing a certain stoicism, fitting on a "Just because you're my mother doesn't mean I have to come to you with all my problems" attitude. I might still live with my parents, still depend on them for all material things, but inside I struggled for independence.

As the days warmed and classes wound down, as I gave in to my boredom and cut a couple of study halls and an English class, faith in my independence swelled. I disregarded the summer plans. I'd simply tell Mom, when she asked, that I'd thought about it and wouldn't mind visiting Grandma for a week, but really, I'd just as soon stay home. I'd dangle the bait of a summer job, too.

She brought it up when I got home Friday afternoon, three weeks after the prom. She was in the kitchen putting groceries away, and I was fixing myself a snack of milk and chocolate chip cookies.

"Have you thought about going to Pittsburgh?" she asked.

"I have, and"—I took a deep breath—"I'd really just as soon stay here, Mom." I put the milk away, my back to her. "I'd be happy to visit Grandma for a week or so, but . . ." I shut the refrigerator door and turned. She was across the room, slapping ground meat she'd just bought into hamburger patties and not looking at me. "But I think I'd be really bored and not have a good time, and that wouldn't be fun for either me or Grandma."

"I think you'll be bored here." She ripped off a length of wax paper. "You told me last week that Karen will be in the Poconos most of the summer, and won't Denny be working full-time at his father's repair shop? What will you do here?"

13

She looked up as she wrapped the hamburgers, her gaze surprisingly flat. If I didn't know her better, I'd say she was holding back tears. But my mom, the eternal optimist, never cried.

After a moment, she looked back down at the hamburgers and stuffed them into a plastic bag. "Think about your grandmother," she went on. "She's lonely out there. She has some friends, and the minister visits her every week, but with Grandpa gone, she can't get out as easily as she used to, and of course there's no one to talk to at home. You'd be good company for her."

"But, Mom." I moved aside as she carried the hamburgers to the refrigerator. "I know Grandma must be lonely, but how can you expect me to spend a whole summer with her?" I appealed to her own frustration with her mother. "Could you? You know that you sometimes get annoyed by her chattering and—and her stubbornness and . . . all that."

I couldn't express exactly how Grandma annoyed all of us without being cruel and sounding as though I didn't like her at all. I did. She was just . . . annoying.

Mom slammed the freezer door shut and turned toward me. The look on her face made me look down. "She is my mother, your grandmother, and I don't like your tone of voice, Ginnie. Whatever faults Grandma has, she is one of the kindest, most loving people I know. You've been telling me for months how grown-up you are and how you want me to treat you as though you're no longer a child. Well, one of the responsibilities of an adult is taking care of her family, and doing it selflessly. Your grandmother needs you, and frankly I think it would be good for you to spend more time with her. You don't really know her that well, and you might discover that she's not nearly as 'annoying' as you think."

"Mom, I didn't mean it. I know she's a nice person, and I'd never want to hurt her." I tried to look at her, but I didn't want her to see how vulnerable I was. "I don't understand why you want me to go out there for the whole summer, though."

She was silent for a long moment, then she sighed and said, "Let's sit down." I followed her into the dining room and slouched down into my chair. She sat in Dad's chair at the head of the table. She nervously tapped her fingers on the tabletop, then stood and fished out a cigarette from the covered bowl on the sideboard. After lighting it, she returned to the table.

"Ginnie . . . " She reached out and lightly touched my arm. I looked up at her. "You know I was only twenty-one when I married, right out of college. And then I got pregnant with Tom just a couple of weeks later. So for the past twenty years I've spent most of my time taking care of you and Tom and your father and this house."

Yes, I knew that. My parents had met in college; she was in her senior year at the University of Pittsburgh—majoring in French and hoping to teach it—and he was in his fourth year, taking what courses he could manage while he worked to support himself.

They met in the fall, and Mom brought him home for dinner sometime after the new year. Grandma didn't like him at first. Not that Dad's table manners were bad, but he hadn't lived the straight-path life Grandma expected of all people. He'd dropped out of high school; he'd been in the military; he'd lived in a YMCA in New York City while trying to make it as an actor. And he kept having to take semesters off from college when his money ran out. He was charming, though, and smart, and after they married that autumn, Grandma—of course—wouldn't say a negative thing about him.

Their first years of marriage, while Dad tried to find a job he liked and Mom took care of two babies, were spent in tiny apartments, with no car until after I was born. Mom would joke that if she'd known how to sew, she would have taken in work, but as it was, she had no choice but to be a mother and housewife.

Maybe if she hadn't had Tom and me, she would have gone back to school to take the education courses she needed to get her teaching certificate. But she did have us, and she used her French only to teach us that language. Even our bedtime stories were sometimes in French, like *Le Petit Prince*. But none of our friends knew French, and they'd make fun of us and her when we spoke it. So by the time he was eight and I was five, Tom and I refused to use French at all, and left her to read her French novels alone at night.

Our life-style improved when I was three and Dad got a job at an insurance company in Philadelphia. They bought the house and joined suburbia, a bridge club, and the PTA.

When I'd confide in Dad that I wanted to study acting and then do what he had done—go live in New York and try to make it big—he'd tell me that having a steady job and a family was more important than trying to live out romantic notions and dreams. Mom would back him up, and she never told me until I was fifteen that she'd tried to be a writer, when Tom and I were still preschoolers. She'd write stories while we napped, then send them off and get every one back with a rejection letter.

She did work some while I was growing up. She got into politics when I started school, and for years around election time Tom and I would wander strange neighborhoods, handing out flyers. But then she voted for Anderson in 1980—Dad voted for Reagan—and she dropped out of politics.

She started planning our elaborate summer vacations then, camping all across the country, and took adult classes at Temple University. Then she got a job as a secretary for a travel agent. We got a trip to Bermuda out of that, but she hated sitting at a desk, talking on the phone all day. She asked my father over dinner one night how he could stand it, the same routine, the same office, day after day, and he said that you have to find satisfaction in your work and fill out the rest of your life with hobbies, as he did with his photography. He sounded like he was lecturing her, which I thought pretty strange, one parent lecturing another. Mom didn't seem to like it, either, because for once she didn't say anything back.

Grandma added her two cents, too, when she and Grandpa came for Christmas a few months later, telling Mom that surely her life was full enough without a job. Mom made some comment about not being the church committee type, at which Grandma got all huffy, saying that serving the community was the finest work anyone could do, which made Grandpa hoot and say that all the women on her church committee were more interested in gossip than in service. Which made us all laugh and Grandma purse her mouth, straighten her spine, and maintain a hurt silence.

Mom got into real estate next, just last year, and that nearly got us a new home. Every Saturday for two months she dragged me along with her to check out houses being built in grassless, treeless stretches of mud, or older homes up for sale. Something was wrong with all of them, and the burst of energy that had enlivened Mom that spring fizzled in the humid summer heat. We didn't buy a new house. When the weather cooled again, she turned her attentions to the house we already had and proceeded to redecorate each room, even building new cabinets herself for the kitchen.

Mom tapped ash into the ashtray. "Now that Tom's pretty much moved out and you're growing up so fast, my life is changing. And, of course, your father's." She tried knocking more ash off, but there wasn't enough. "He and I have been talking, and we—" She took a deep drag on the cigarette. Now there was ash, and I watched as she flicked it into the ashtray, then moved it around with the tip of the cigarette. "We feel we need some time to get back in touch with each other, and with what we want. We've both grown and changed over the past twenty years, and what we want for ourselves now is different from what we wanted when we were twenty-one."

Well, of course, I thought, but I still didn't understand why she was telling me this. She saw that. Sighing again, she stubbed out the cigarette and turned her full focus on me.

"What I'm saying, Ginnie, is that we need to be alone

for a little while." She smiled. "Sort of like a second honeymoon. We need to concentrate on just ourselves, see where we want our marriage to go."

I mulled over that last statement. How did marriages go anywhere? They just were, weren't they? There were children and a house, and then when the children left for college and their own lives, the parents still had the house and their jobs and hobbies, and they bought a motor home and took long vacations together. Why did they have to be alone to figure out where they were *going*?

"Ginnie, I know this is difficult for you to understand. You know what it's like to be part of a family, but you don't know what it's like to be part of a couple. Marriage is not . . . just living together, and it's not easy. The two people have to work together toward certain goals, and they have to give each other room to grow in whatever direction . . ."

She looked away from me, out the back window where the lilac trees were in full flower and the apple tree was covered in white blossoms. I didn't bother puzzling over what she had just said; I wasn't interested in what it meant to be married. I wanted to hear specifics about her and Dad. Why was their marriage not easy?

She didn't say, though. She drew herself back and looked at me. "I'm not explaining myself very well, but, Ginnie, it's important for your father and me to have this time alone together. And it's just as important for your grandmother not to be alone, and for you to get to know her better." She smiled, but for a woman whose wide mouth usually curved into wide smiles, this was a pretty poor one. "Don't think that your father and I don't love you anymore, and that we're sending you off to punish you. We do love you, and I know we'll miss you very much. But it won't be for long. Consider it a trial run for college."

I managed a wispy smile of my own. I'd sort out later all that she said, but for now I simply gave in. She'd left me no choice. She'd taken away that tiny bit of independence I'd forged for myself. Without speaking, only nodding my head to show I'd heard her and wouldn't fight her anymore, I stood, picked up my milk and chocolate chip cookies, and went upstairs. I turned my radio on as loud as I could stand it—which was much louder than she could stand it—and didn't reappear until dinner. When I did, we didn't talk about the summer, marriage, or Pittsburgh. Mom just told me Dad and I would drive out to Grandma's Saturday, June twenty-fourth, a week and a half after school ended.

THREE

So how was your first day in Pittsburgh?" my mother asks when she calls Sunday evening.

I hold the phone away from my ear. My mother's forceful voice may be wonderful for calling kids in for dinner, but over the phone it is irritating, too loud and direct.

"It was fine, Mom."

"Just 'fine'? What did you do?"

"Well, Grandma said it was okay if I worked in her garden, so I did that."

"And?"

"And I finished the book I was reading."

We are both silent for a minute. Silence has hung between us most of the time since I agreed to come to Pittsburgh.

She mentions the weather, how hot it is there.

I tell her it's hot here, too.

She says Dad said I drove very well yesterday.

"Yeah, for thirty whole minutes," I say.

She laughs, but the sound is forced. I hold the phone away again.

"It's nice to hear your voice," she says. "Already the house seems empty without you."

I don't respond. After all, it wasn't my idea to leave.

"Put your grandmother on," Mom says into the silence. "I'll say good-bye to you now and call you again in a few days."

"Okay. 'Bye."

I set the phone on the sofa cushion, walk to the foot of the stairs, and call up to Grandma that Mom's on the phone.

"All right," Grandma's voice floats down.

I return to the sofa and pick up the phone, holding it with the listening part to my ear and the speaking part above my head.

"Hello, Claire," my grandmother's voice trills. I can hear her in stereo, over the phone and from upstairs.

"Hello, Mother," my mother says. "How are you?"

"Oh, I'm just fine, dear. And how are you?"

"I'm good, considering the heat."

"I *know*. Isn't it just *dreadful* . . ."

More weather talk. Then Grandma asks if Dad got home okay.

Mom says of course, and adds that he said the dinner Grandma served last night was delicious, as usual.

Grandma laughs. "I guess it must have been. He had

seconds of everything. He truly is a wonderful man, Claire. I was so *pleased* when I first met him, and I haven't been disappointed yet."

There is a long pause, then Mom asks, "How are you getting along with Ginnie? Everything okay?"

"Oh, of *course*! I love having her here. She's so sweet and darling. She made dinner tonight and washed all the dishes."

"She did, huh? Did Richard leave you enough money?"

"Too much! I tried to give it back to him. I'm sure I can afford to feed my own granddaughter."

"Two months is a long time, Mother."

"Oh no, not really. I'm sure the time will just whiz by. And Ginnie worked in the back garden for hours this afternoon. I'm so glad she's willing to do that. You know, I really haven't been able to do much gardening myself these past few years. It's those steps," she adds quickly. "They aren't quite safe. They're a little loose. It's not that I couldn't do the *work*." She laughs as if her daughter had accused her of just that. "Why, I'm as spry as I was when you were born. But it will be nice to have someone working in the garden again. And Ginnie's such a good little gardener. That is something the three of us have in common."

"I guess we do. Let Ginnie use Father's car at your discretion. She's a good driver. And remember to call me if anything goes wrong."

"Oh, Claire. You really shouldn't worry so."

Knowing my mother is about to end the conversation, I gently put down the phone. By the time I hear Grandma descending the stairs, I'm in the kitchen scooping out ice cream. I've already filled a bowl with chocolate for myself and am about to drop some vanilla in a glass for her.

"How about a ginger ale float, Grandma?" I call as she crosses the living room.

"Oh, that would be wonderful, Ginnie."

I plop two scoops of vanilla into the tall glass, then fill it with frothy ginger ale. I hand her the glass and a long spoon.

"Why don't we eat this out in the backyard?" she says. "It must be cooler out there."

The night is still and quiet, although it is just past nine o'clock. Some cicadas hum, a car and a bus pass, but otherwise it is silent. Grandma and I sit on lawn chairs and scoop up our ice cream. Its coldness shivers through me in the oppressive, humid heat.

We say nothing for several minutes, then Grandma sighs and sets her glass on the round metal table beside her. "It's nights like these," she says, "when I miss your grandfather the most. We used to sit out here in the evening, listening to the ball game, and just enjoying the night air. That's the wonderful thing about marriage, that companionship you share with another person. When you grow up and fall in love, you'll understand what I mean."

I eat more ice cream, silent.

"Your mother," she goes on, "would understand. She's been married to your father for twenty-one years now." She says that with a certain satisfaction, as if she is responsible for every one of those years. "That's a long time. I don't understand why she keeps running out to get a job. She has a job. She's a wife and a mother."

What can I say? If I argue with Grandma, she'll get

24

angry and punish me with silence. If I say nothing, she'll think I agree with her and pass that on to Mom. I try to be evenhanded.

"Well, you know, Grandma, there's not all that much to do around the house anymore. I mean, Tom's hardly ever there now, and I'll be gone in another year. You can't blame her for being a little bored."

"Nonsense. 'Bored.' Hmph. And even if Tom isn't home, that doesn't mean he doesn't still need his mother. What if he tries to call her one day and she's out selling real estate? How is he going to feel?"

I don't point out that Tom is sensible enough to call back, and that Mom could just as easily miss this hypothetical phone call while she's pushing a shopping cart up the aisles of the local Pathmark.

"You need her, too, Ginnie," Grandma continues. "Oh, I know that you young people today think you grow up so fast, leave home when you're eighteen and that's that, you'll never need your parents again. But, oh no, that's not how it works. You never stop needing your parents.

"Why, I remember when I was just a few years older than you . . ."

Her voice drifts effortlessly across the yard, skipping through the petunias and swinging on the trees. It is naturally melodious, rising and falling through an octave as her emotions and memories rise and fall. Although much higher than my mother's voice and deceptively softer, it is just as insistent. I have to strain to stop listening to her words, to hear only the lilting rhythm of her speech, my ear tuned for tonal changes that indicate a switch in subject or a question.

I let my thoughts drift off as her voice does. They wander aimlessly for a while, then I consider how the summer night air, though we're separated from Philadelphia by more than three hundred miles and a set of low, ancient mountains, is so much like the summer night air at home. Nighttime, when Denny comes for me and I barely say good-bye to my parents before straddling his motorcycle, clinging to him as we roar off.

No matter what Mom says about her and Dad "needing a second honeymoon," Denny's got to be part of the reason I'm in Pittsburgh. Mom complains unendingly about the haze and stench of cigarette smoke that hangs around him, tells me that from what she can see, he's too reckless on his motorcycle, and in general questions what I see in him.

I can't explain that it's what he sees in me that matters. That ever since that pool party last summer, he's made me feel attractive and one of the gang, not the perpetual outsider.

A week before that party, Denny had been racing his motorcycle along the few dirt roads remaining in our neighborhood. The bike skidded, throwing him off. A sharp rock gouged into his lower left calf, tearing through jeans and flesh.

At the pool party, he gloried in his wound. Lying back on a lounge chair, his crutches on the concrete beside him, he kept asking girls to get him another soda, some more pretzels, whatever. Many did it gladly, giggling and playing with their hair.

"Hey, Ginnie!" he called to me when there were no

other girls around. "How about getting me a soda?"

I was sitting on my towel not far from him, pretending to read. All around the pool girls were teasing boys, then shrieking and pleading with them as the boys threatened to throw them in the water. I only hoped no boy would maliciously decide my hair was too dry and drag me off into the pool. Not that I didn't like boys or swimming. I just wasn't much good at teasing and shrieking. I preferred silence. And a few cases of agonizing unrequited love had taught me that I was a better friend than potential girlfriend.

So when Denny asked me to get him a soda, I simply looked at him, holding myself stiff, refusing him, his charm. I would not be like the other girls, I told myself.

"Get it yourself," I said.

"Aw, come on, Ginnie. My leg's all torn up and it hurts to walk. Please?"

He smiled, a smile he must have practiced, curiously innocent and endearing, even though everyone knew he was far from innocent. He'd been using that smile to advantage since I had known him, convincing girls to let him copy their homework, write an English paper for him, loan him some money, go out with him. He'd never used that smile on me.

"What do you want another soda for?" I asked. "You've already had six or so."

"Come here," he said, leaning forward, "and I'll tell you a secret."

I walked over to him, carrying my towel, since several unguarded ones had already landed in the water. Standing over him, I asked, "What?"

27

He motioned for me to bend down. I did, wondering if the top of my one-piece suit gaped away from my body, revealing my small breasts. If it did, Denny didn't look. He cupped one hand around his mouth and whispered, "I only finished two of those sodas."

I pulled back. "Then why'd you ask for them?"

He grinned and shrugged. "It's fun having all these girls wait on me."

"It's not very nice." I draped the towel around my shoulders like a shawl, holding it closed in front of me.

"Why not?" he asked. "They wanted to do it."

A giggling squeal cut the air, followed by a splash and a boy's laugh. I looked up to see my best friend's head bob to the surface. Karen shook her fist at the boy who'd thrown her in, a boy she'd had a crush on for most of the year.

I glanced back down at Denny. "Well, if you didn't drink any of those sodas, why do you want me to get you another one?"

He shrugged and fiddled with the gold chain around his neck. "I just wanted someone to talk to me. It's pretty boring lying here with this wrecked-up leg."

My gaze drifted down his tanned leg. He was wearing only gym shorts and the white bandage wrapped around his calf. I'd heard the wound was gruesome and was glad he wasn't showing it off.

"How long—" I began to ask, but Michelle, head cheerleader and one of the first bleached blondes in our class, bounced over to Denny's chair. Carefully drying herself, she patted the tops of her breasts, then rubbed her stomach and hips, too fleshy to my mind to be

28

exposed in a soggy, skimpy bikini.

"You know, Denny," she said in her flat Kansas voice as she toweled her hair, "it's too bad you have to just sit here in the sun. The water is so nice."

"Aw, it's okay, Michelle. Besides, the scenery's pretty good."

Michelle smiled, revealing straight white teeth. "You're such a flirt, Denny."

The comment could have been slighting, but of course wasn't. Michelle thrived on attention from men. I didn't think she was attractive, with her plump belly and over-bleached strawlike hair, but she had something the boys liked—breasts. When she'd transferred to our school in ninth grade, she'd had the largest breasts of any girl in the class. She still did.

She dropped her towel and posed, one hip jutted out, her stomach sucked in, and asked him if his leg hurt much, and wasn't it just *awful* when it happened?

He agreed—awful; but you know, he was more worried about his bike.

She cooed about the poor bike, poor Denny, the crutches, the bandage. "Will you have to keep the bandage on all summer?"

"Just another month," he told her. "It's healing real well. Wanna see?"

She stepped back. "Uh . . ."

"I'd like to see," I said.

He grinned slyly at me, then sat up and reached for the bandage. Michelle picked up her towel, holding it in front of her. We watched Denny.

Scabbed-over scrapes and cuts surrounded a thick,

square pad held onto the inside of his leg by white tape. He hid a wince as he tugged the tape free, then pulled the pad up.

I tried not to see, focusing on the back of the pad instead of the wound. Still, I saw enough. His leg did have a hole in it, more than an inch in diameter, the flesh around it ragged and raw.

"That's *disgusting*!" Michelle cried out. "How could you show me something like that? I'm probably going to have nightmares tonight!"

He shrugged. "Seen enough, Ginnie?"

I drew back. "Sure."

"You two," Michelle pronounced, "are both sick."

She turned and stalked off. As she neared the pool, a boy ran up behind her and yelled, "Hey, Michelle!" She looked back, and he pushed her into the water. She managed to get rid of her towel just in time.

I watched as she surfaced, spluttering and screaming; then I grinned and glanced down at Denny. He was gazing at me with a curious intentness.

"Hey, Ginnie," he said. "Want a cigarette?"

F O U R

June 27

Dear Ginnie,
*Eleven o'clock Tuesday night and it is still unbear-
ably hot here in Philadelphia. The humidity is the
worst, but it always is. I imagine it's just as bad in Pittsburgh.
I remember those sticky summers when I was growing up.*

*At least your father and I got a bit of a break this evening.
We went out to dinner and then to see a play at the Walnut
Street Theater. Your father's thinking of working part-time at
the camera store again this summer. They've told him they can
use him 6:30 to 9:30 Tuesday and Friday nights. It's not for
the money, you know. It's a good change of pace for him, and it
gives him the chance to talk about his favorite hobby with other
people.*

*Not much is happening on the street. Doris was over
yesterday, telling me that Roberta is finally dating someone*

and may actually be serious about the guy. Doris didn't say so, but she probably can't wait for Roberta to get a place of her own.

Speaking of children, Tom called right after I talked to you Sunday night. He'd had to take one of the campers back to the base camp. The boy just couldn't handle it, the canoeing, the camping. Tom sounded good and promised he would write as often as possible. He said the black flies are fierce up there this year. Everyone's practically taking showers in Old Woodsman, that awful-smelling bug spray.

The house is so quiet tonight. I almost miss you playing your radio loud enough to burst my eardrums, let alone your own. Sometimes I think the choruses of your favorite songs are embedded in my brain on permanent sound tracks. I just wish I understood them better. I mean, is "Losing My Religion" really about losing religion?

It's cooling off a little now, so I guess I'll go to bed. Though since you're not here, maybe I'll take the coolest spot in the house for a change and sleep on the couch.

It's so quiet out there.

Love,
Mom

"How's your mother?" Grandma asks.

I set the letter down and push myself up out of Grandpa's deep armchair. "She's fine. She says it's still hot there."

Grandma nods and sips her iced tea. It's still hot here, too, a thick, humid heat that drains my energy. I sweat simply walking down to the garden. The heat's heaviness settles not just in my arms and legs, but in my head. For a week I've only read and gardened, and listened to

Grandma recreate the past. Every day she suggests I go across the street to the Webers', who have seven children, and find someone to do something with, but I never do. Too much effort.

I stare out the front screen door, my eyes unfocused so that the thin, crooked branches of the cherry tree in the front yard resemble the witches' arms that reached for me in my childhood nightmares. The rest of the summer is stretching out before me like a hot, stifling tunnel that winds endlessly through a black mountain. No way out. No chance to turn around and stop.

No one is asking me to dinner, I think as a heavy cloud presses down on my brain, or to the theater. Is that what they're going to do all summer? Have fun, while I sweat and pull weeds and read until I have a headache? I doubt that they're worried about their marriage "going" some-place. They just couldn't wait until I was finally gone.

I turn from the door. "I'm going to go outside to write letters, Grandma."

She is silent for a moment, her thin lips pressed together, then she sighs and nods. I try to force aside an anxious fear that, unable to find the energy or desire to be cheerful and entertaining, I am disappointing her horribly.

July 1

Dear Mom,

It seems silly to write to you today (Saturday) when I'll probably talk to you tomorrow, but I figured I should answer your letter.

I haven't done much all week. Took Grandma shopping a few times. Driving Grandpa's Dodge is fun, but I'm glad I

*learned to drive on Grandpa Ryan's Bonneville. The Dodge is
a little smaller, so it's actually easier to drive. I'm still figuring
out how to tell where my right wheel is, though.*

*I've been helping out around the house a lot. I wash the
dishes every day. Yesterday I vacuumed, and the day before I
polished all the wood furniture. I told Grandma I'd wash the
windows too when it's a little cooler.*

*We're pretty hot here, although they're predicting thunder-
storms this afternoon. I've gone to the pool a couple of times, but
that's not much fun alone. Grandma keeps telling me to go over
to the Webers', but I feel kind of silly, like a little girl who
doesn't have anyone to play with. I'm reading a lot, and
Grandma lets me use Grandpa's portable radio, so at least I can
listen to music up in my room. Her cassette player still sits on the
piano bench in the living room, but when I played my REM
tape the other day, Grandma looked like she was in such pain, I
turned it off.*

*You know, Mom, if you really listened to the songs, I think
you'd understand them. They're just about life, about the mess
this world is in. I left some of my tapes there. Listen to the one
by Tracy Chapman. Or Suzanne Vega. Listen to the words,
about how we all hurt each other.*

*That's your lecture for the day. Is Dad really going to work
at the camera store again? I remember last summer he used to
get home real late, and the next morning he'd always com-
plain about how tired he was.*

*I guess since I'm not there it's okay that you take the
couch. I've never been able to figure out why it's so much
cooler down there, because I've got a window that faces south
too, but it never gets that same breeze.*

I think I'll go to the pool this afternoon, maybe stay there

*until the thunderstorms come and then walk home in the rain.
That'll keep me cool. Remember how I used to think rain
clouds were witches flying across the sky on broomsticks?*

I drop the letter onto the ground beside my lawn chair.
Should I have written that bit about the couch? Or Dad's
working . . .

"Ginnie!" Grandma calls through the back screen
door. "Kris is here."

I look up, shading my eyes with my hand. "Who?"

She makes a little sound of annoyance, then the door
opens and she steps outside. Dressed in grass green today,
she outshines the white bricks of the house. "You know,"
she whispers. "Kris Weber. From across the street."

"Oh. Him."

With a slowness that would tempt my mother to throw
something at me, I ease off the lawn chair. Pulling one of
my dad's discarded white shirts on over my bathing suit, I
trudge toward the house. "Where is he?"

"He's out front. You hurry on upstairs and put something on, and I'll tell him you'll be right down."

"What's wrong with what I'm wearing?"

"Honestly!" She shoos me inside. "You go right on upstairs and put on something nice. And comb your hair.
And get rid of those ridiculous sunglasses. You have very
pretty eyes and you shouldn't hide them like that."

"The sun's too bright not to wear them."

"You shouldn't be sitting in the sun anyway. It'll ruin
your skin."

I don't argue anymore, but head upstairs. I haven't
seen Kris in a few years, and try to remember what he

35

looks like. All I can recall is that he is blond like his sister Alta, who is my age. He's a year or two younger than me.

Not about to put on "something nice," I unearth from my mother's suitcase a cropped top and shorts. Downstairs I hear her open the front door and let Kris in. She asks about his family, but I can't hear his answer. I change quickly, wondering what I'll say to him.

Downstairs, Grandma is posed in her tapestried wing chair and a boy is leaning forward on the couch, bony elbows on bony knees. When I reach the bottom of the stairs, he stands up. His arms dangle oddly at his sides, too long even for his gangly frame. His hair has darkened from a pale blond to a sandy color with lighter streaks. His pale-blue eyes under pale brows are curiously blank.

"Hi," he says. "Would you like to go to the pool?"

I glance at Grandma, who smiles and bobs her head. I know what she's thinking. Anyone is better than Denny. "I have to get my towel and suit," I say to Kris.

He nods and plops back down on the couch.

I roll my bathing suit and cigarettes into my beach towel, grab a few dollars, and slip on my new rubber sandals. I am at the top of the stairs when I remember I need a book to read. Scanning the collection in my bedroom, I decide a Lord Peter Wimsey mystery will do. I reach down to pick one up, then impulsively grab a Travis McGee instead. Not that I like Travis McGee better, but I think its cover drawing of a naked woman, lying on her stomach with a towel draped over her backside, will be good for effect.

We say good-bye to Grandma and leave. I wait for Kris to say we're driving there, but he walks to the sidewalk without speaking and turns down the hill.

"Wait a minute," I say. "We're walking?"

His eyes have no expression as he looks at me. "How else?"

"Well, it's kind of a long way." It's how I've gotten there all week, and it's no fun in the heat. "You can't borrow your mother's car?"

"She's using it. And walking is good exercise." He glances at my sandals. "You should wear sneakers, though."

Of course I should. "These are really comfortable." This is going to be a long, lousy afternoon.

He shrugs. "Okay. There are a couple of shortcuts we can take, so it's not that far."

You wanted something to do, I tell myself as I follow him. Now you have something to do. It takes nearly half an hour to walk each way. What are we going to talk about?

"How's Alta?" I ask.

"She's in London."

"You're kidding! London? What's she doing there?"

"Working. She was studying over there this spring on a special program, and she decided to stay for the summer. The head of the study program helped her get a job as a maid in a hotel."

The romance of working in a hotel in London eclipses the prestige of dating a guy who rides a motorcycle. Instantly, a fantasy spins through my mind. There I am, making the bed in a luxurious suite, when a man, a lord or an earl, maybe Lord Peter Wimsey, comes in. He needs my help. He's just found incriminating evidence that will send a traitor to prison, but he's being followed. I must get the evidence to the Prime Minister. He hands me an envelope . . .

"Nicole's in Russia," Kris says.

"Huh?"

"My sister Nicole? She's in Russia."

"Oh." I remember there are three or four girls in this family, and Nicole is the oldest. "Why is she in Russia?"

"She's studying there. She's been there since last October. She'll be coming home in a couple of weeks."

"What about your other sisters? Where are they?"

"At home." His tone implies there is no other place they could be. "Cara's only fourteen, and Ian and Aileen are nine and eight."

"Right." I'd forgotten about those two youngest ones. "How come you aren't overseas?"

"Not this year," he answers seriously. "I'll probably go next year, after I graduate from high school."

I glance at him. "You're going to be a senior this year?" He nods. "Oh, then you're my age."

"No, Alta's your age. I'm a year younger. I'm just graduating early."

I realize I'm not only sounding stupid, I'm feeling stupid. No one has offered me the chance to go to Europe, or to graduate early. Kids at my school think I'm brainy, but also cool because I date Denny. Compared to Kris and his sisters, I'm dull. I regret bringing the Travis McGee book. Kris is probably reading Dickens or Hemingway. As we continue along the hard sidewalk, sweat prickling under my arms and down my back, I think that no matter how much I try, I'm an awkward person, unable to fit in.

The pool is crowded. Despite the promise of thundershowers, it is miserably hot.

Kris and I pay our money and go to our respective

38

locker rooms. I change in a toilet stall. My feet are sore and tender, so I leave the sandals in a locker with my shorts and top. I take the cigarettes and book with me.

Kris is waiting for me by the exit to the girls' locker room. He's wearing only his trunks, and I'm embarrassed by his bare chest, so thin and pale.

"How about over there?" he asks, pointing to the far end of the pool.

"Fine."

We spread our towels on the grassy incline and sit. He stares at the diving board while I slather on suntan lotion.

"Do you have a girlfriend?" I ask. I don't really care, but I want to let him know I have a boyfriend.

"No," he says. "I'm not interested in dating. There are more important things to do."

I wipe my hands on the grass. "Yeah? Like what?"

He shrugs. "Just things."

"I have a boyfriend. Denny Cunningham." I slip into my "Denny's girlfriend" role. "He's probably going to be coming out here this summer. He has a motorcycle."

Kris looks at me. "Your mother doesn't mind your going out with him?"

I laugh. "She hates it. But in front of my grandmother she'll defend to the death my right to date him. And Grandma takes every chance she can to tell me how bad he is for me, how he'll ruin my 'reputation.'" I pitch my voice high, imitating her.

"Your grandmother's a nice woman."

"You're not spending the summer with her. Of course, it's better than spending the summer with my parents."

I figure this is the perfect moment to light a cigarette,

a final touch to my scorn. But looking around, I'm not sure smoking is allowed. And goody-two-shoes Kris might tell Grandma.

"Don't you like anybody?" he asks.

"Sure. I like my boyfriend. But, shit, you don't expect me to like my *parents*, do you?"

I cringe at my words. I've cribbed them from some teenage rebellion movie and they sound absurd and false. Quickly I ask, "Do you like your parents?"

He shrugs again. "They're not so bad. I don't feel I have to fight with them."

"I fight with my mother all the time."

"Really?" He turns to face me. "You yell at her?"

"Oh, no. No one in my house raises their voice. I guess . . ."

I stop. How do I fight with her? How does she fight with Dad? No one shouts, no one calls anyone names. No one slams doors or stays out all night. But maybe that's the way we fight. Maybe we keep our anger tight around ourselves, a barrier to any closeness or forgiveness.

"You guess what?" Kris asks.

"I guess we don't fight. We just don't talk."

"You have to talk. That's how you resolve problems."

"Well, excuse me!" I exclaim, infuriated by his tone. "I'm sorry if my family isn't perfect like yours. Sorry my brother and I aren't studying overseas. Sorry—sorry I came along."

I could stand right then and stalk off, trailing cigarettes and Travis McGee. But I stay, not knowing how to make a dramatic exit. He stares at me, bewilderment in his pale eyes, and I almost apologize.

40

Instead, I start to cry. I can't believe it. I never cry. I
never cry. My throat tightens. My eyes burn. I turn away
and fumble for my cigarettes, not caring if I get kicked
out. Wanting to get kicked out. Wanting to be bad and to
not care that I've let anyone down.

The match stays lit in the windless air, and my shaking
hand gets it to the cigarette.

"I didn't mean to upset you," Kris mumbles.

"I'm all right." I blow out the match and wipe tears
from my face. "I'm all right."

I smoke and imagine my anger is like the cigarette,
glowing brighter and fiercer with each concentrated drag.
The anger locks onto my mother. It's her fault I'm here.

The tip of the cigarette flares red, then fades to gray as
I suck in another lungful. Maybe I'm better away. I don't
want to know what they're doing while I'm gone. I don't
care. They can go to the theater every night. They can
buy a damn motor home. I don't care.

I'm better off here. No one knows me, and Grandma
won't keep as close tabs on me as Mom. Freedom, more
independence. Now is my chance to form myself without
Mom constantly watching, criticizing. Now I can find all
the different sides to myself, try them on and see which
fit best, feel best.

Yes, I'm glad I'm here, away from them. They can play
with their marriage. I don't care.

I exhale smoke. Don't care. Inhale smoke. They don't
matter. Exhale smoke. Don't care . . .

F I V E

Dear Denny,
    The days go by so slowly here in Pittsburgh. I can't believe I've only been here little more than a week. It feels as if it must have been a month by now.

    I don't do much. I get up around seven, which means Grandma has already been up for an hour or two, puttering around in the kitchen. We have breakfast and then I do some housework for her. Just how I wanted to spend my summer, doing housework. Then the rest of the day is mine. I've been reading a lot. I've been going to the pool, too. It's a long walk, but Grandma won't let me use Grandpa's car unless she's with me.

    You should see this car, Denny. You'd love it. It's a 1963 Dodge, white. It's huge and really classy-looking. I feel like everyone's looking at us when we drive to the store in it.

So what are you doing? Do you have to work in your dad's store every day, or is he giving you some time off? Do you see much of Mark and Randy? Are Sue and Mike still going out? Tell them all I said hi.

I'm writing this in my bedroom, and it's starting to get really warm. I don't know how I always end up with the hottest bedroom in the house. So I'll finish this and take it up the street to mail it. I need to buy more cigarettes, and that's not something I can do when I'm with Grandma.

I hope you're okay, and that you don't have an accident like you did last summer. One scar's enough.

I sit up on the bed and debate, again, how to sign the letter. I had the same problem when I wrote him a week ago. Back in April, Denny told me he'd fallen in love with me, but I've never said the same to him. So I don't want to sign the letter "Love," like I would with my parents and girlfriends.

Finally I write "I miss you," like I did last time, add my name, then fold the letter and slip it into an envelope. I'm about to seal it when I take the letter back out and reread it.

Boredom seeps from every word I've written, not the excitement Denny arouses in me. Lying on my back, I picture him hovering over me, as if he were about to kiss me. I can see the tousled dark hair, the half smile, the gold chain that dangles down and brushes my chin. The eyes are hazy, though, and I can't get the line of his jaw right. I try to pretend he's kissing me, but I only feel foolish, playing pretend like a little girl.

I roll over and stuff the letter back into the envelope,

sealing it inside. "Denny," I whisper, wishing he could hear, wishing I had the nerve to call him, "I'm lonely. I need to be with you. I need to hear you tell me you love me."

I sit motionless for a moment, then push myself off the bed and head downstairs, the letter and some money in my shorts pocket. I'll mail the letter up at the top of the street, where all the stores are. Sneaking two or three cigarettes a day, I've finished the pack Denny jokingly gave me as a going-away gift.

"Grandma!" I call as I reach the living room. "I'm going for a walk."

"All right, dear," she answers from the kitchen. "Are you going with Kris?"

I swallow a groan. She's asked that every time I've left the house for the past three days, ever since Kris and I went to the pool together. "No, I'm not going with Kris. You know, Grandma, Kris and I don't get along all that well."

She walks from the kitchen into the dining room, bumping the table as she comes to an unsteady stop.

"How can you say that?" she asks. "He's a very nice boy."

"We don't have anything in common. He's interested in science and stuff."

"Well, heavens." She laughs. "Of course you're interested in different things. He's a boy. He's not going to like the same things you do."

"I'll be back in a little while," I say, and leave.

After days of unusual heat, we've had days of unusual coolness. The sun is warm, but whenever clouds roll

44

across it I wish I'd worn jeans. Still I am hot enough by the time I climb to the top of the steep hill. Cars zip past, and the sidewalk is crowded with mothers and children and wandering teenagers.

A drugstore sits on the corner of Grandma's street, a mailbox in front of it. I drop Denny's letter into the box, then go inside the store. Behind the counter in the front are cartons of cigarettes stacked six feet up. I can just walk up to one of the registers and ask for a pack of Marlboros. That's what Denny smokes, so that's what I smoke. But I've never bought cigarettes before, always smoking his or stealing my mother's, and I turn away from the counter. Maybe I should buy something else, too.

I stroll down the first aisle, stopping to flip through some address books. Hearing a giggle on the other side, I walk to the end of the aisle and peer around the corner. Three girls my age are standing by a jewelry display, holding earrings up to their faces.

"These are wild," one says, studying her reflection in a pocket mirror. "I'm gonna take these."

"Shh!" another hisses. "Not so loud. We might get kicked out of here again."

The first one gives her a bored look and snaps her gum. "You know, you can just leave now."

"Come on," the third one says. "Just take the earrings and get outta here."

The first girl drops her pocket mirror and the earrings into her massive shoulder bag. Even if she gets stopped, I think, no one would ever find those earrings. They turn and start toward the door, but the first girl glances back and sees me. Her eyes, heavily rimmed with black liner, narrow suspiciously.

"Hey!" she calls quietly. "What are you doing?"

I shrug. "Nothing."

She walks toward me, silver bracelets jangling. "You better not tell anyone what you saw."

"I didn't see anything. I only came in here to buy some cigarettes."

That stops her. She studies me from head to foot, no doubt comparing my chin-length straight brown hair with her long, frizzy reddish-blond mass; my childish cotton shorts and shirt with her black camisole top and short tight skirt.

"The cigarettes are up front, behind the counter," she says, her voice harsh but not mean.

I nod. "I was just looking around."

"I've never seen you before. Did you just move here?"

"No. I'm spending the summer with my grandmother. I'm from Philadelphia."

Once more her gaze slides over me. She reaches into her bag, fumbles inside for a moment, then pulls out a pack of cigarettes. Marlboros in the red-and-white crush-proof box. "What kinda cigs do you smoke?"

"Kents."

Why did I say that? I want to smoke something different from her, but Kents? That's what my mother smokes.

"Yeah?" She taps out a cigarette and lights it with the lighter she kept inside the crush-proof box. "Well, why don't you go get some?"

She and her friends stand between me and the cash registers. As I start forward, I estimate how much room I have to squeeze past them, knowing they won't move over. I have almost reached her when a man calls loudly behind me, "Hey, you girls!"

My shoulders hunch inward and I glance back. A man about my father's age, wearing a pale-blue smock, stands a few feet away, glaring at us.

"If you're not going to buy anything," he says, "get out of the store. And there's no smoking in here."

The girl beside me stares back at him, blowing out a long plume of smoke. Then she jerks her head to the other two.

"Come on," she says. "Everything in this store is junk anyway."

The three head toward the exit. I turn my back on the man and pretend to examine the fake gold necklaces.

"You too," he says. "Get out of here. I know you girls steal jewelry all the time, and if I ever catch one of you at it, I'm going to see you thrown in jail."

I try to mimic the other girls' nonchalance as I give him a quick look, then dart down the aisle and out the door. The girls are one store away and I shout after them, "Thanks a lot!"

They turn and stare, and the first girl walks back to me. "Did he kick you out too?"

"Yeah. Now where am I supposed to get my cigarettes?"

"Shit. You can get cigarettes tons of places. Come on. I'll show you where Lenny's is."

Lenny's is long and narrow and smoky. It doesn't belong on that street of middle-class shops, the butchers and the florists and the bookstore and the hair salon. At first all I see are stacks of newspapers on one side and a long counter on the other, behind which are hundreds of cartons of cigarettes and large, square jars of tobacco. Hearing noise in the back, I peer around the other girls. Two video machines, a soda machine, a cigarette machine, and a couple of tables and chairs fill the back half. Two boys are playing the video machines, their bodies lean and taut and jerking as they thrust the joysticks back and forth.

"You can get your cigarettes here," the red-blond girl says to me, nodding toward the cigarette machine.

My hands in my pockets, I stroll to the back of the store, past the two boys playing the video games. Neither of them looks at me.

I dig all my change out of my pocket and start dropping coins into the slot. Scanning the miniature cigarette packs above each plastic knob, I spot the Kents. I let the last dime slide down into the slot, make sure I have the right knob, and pull. The machine chugs, clunks, and the white pack of cigarettes and a packet of matches drop onto the narrow shelf at the bottom. I scoop them out.

The red-blond girl is standing beside me. "By the way, my name's Diane."

"I'm Ginnie."

She nods. "That's Cheryl." She points at the chunky brown-haired girl who'd been nervous in the drugstore. "And that's Barbara." Barbara has long dark hair and ice-green eyes.

We all say hi. Diane drops her bag on the floor and fishes out her new earrings. "What d'ya think of these?" she asks as she inserts them into the tiny holes in her ears.

They are long, thin black spirals, and wisps of her hair curl around them.

"They're great," I say.

Cheryl moves closer to examine the earrings, but Diane turns, saying she wants a soda. We trail after her to the soda machine. The three of them get Cokes, and look at me skeptically when I tell them I don't like soda. I light a cigarette.

"So what should we do?" Diane asks.

"We could go to the pool," Cheryl says.

Barbara and Diane give her identical looks of boredom.

"It's getting hot again," Cheryl adds.

"Maybe if you lost some weight," Barbara says, "you wouldn't be so hot all the time."

Her casual cruelty stuns me. I turn away as Cheryl stares at the floor.

"Knock it off, Barbara," Diane says. "God, you can be such a bitch."

Barbara shrugs. "I'm getting my period."

"What do you do, Ginnie?" Diane asks. "Isn't it boring living with your grandmother?"

"It's no worse than being at home with my parents."

"Yeah, I can see that." Diane finishes her Coke and tosses the can into a wastebasket twenty feet away.

"Oh I'm impressed," Barbara says, and adds to me, "She plays basketball."

"Really?" I try to imagine Diane and the girl jocks at my school on the same team. "I play volleyball myself."

Diane nods. "Volleyball's cool. Maybe if we get enough kids together we could play sometime."

A light appears at the end of the dark tunnel of my summer.

"I play volleyball," Cheryl says.

"Yeah, you're pretty good." Diane glances at Barbara, and I sense a challenge passing between them.

Barbara flicks her long hair over her shoulder and strolls over to the trash can. She drains her soda, tilting her head far back, then drops the can into the basket.

"Hey, Tommy," she calls to the one boy still playing a video game. "Let's go for a drive."

Tommy looks up, letting his spaceship crash. "Where do you want to go?"

"I don't care." She lifts her hair off her neck. "But it's getting hot. It'll be cooler riding in a car."

Tommy grins. "Sure. Let's go."

They start toward the front of Lenny's, Barbara glancing back and smiling at us.

"What a flirt," Diane says. She lights a cigarette, then scrapes a speck of red nail polish off her thumb. "She just better hope her boyfriend doesn't find out. Hey, I got an idea. Let's go to Burger King and get some fries. It's air-conditioned there."

"Great," Cheryl says.

I nod and follow them out of Lenny's. At least for the moment, I have friends.

S I X

ife with Grandma is filled with her voice. Sweet and
melodic, it can be beautiful background music. And
when she merrily babbles on, she is not intruding on
me. She rarely asks me questions, rarely asks about my feelings. She speaks of memories, of people she knew. She
speaks of the past and rarely the present. Never the future.

I sense she was a golden girl, even in the farm country
of Pennsylvania. Petite, with wide blue eyes and a soft
laugh, she must have been attractive. Grandpa was obviously in love. Before they were engaged, when they were
apart for a year, he wrote her every day. She wrote back,
every day, and now keeps all of their letters in shoe boxes
in the bottom dresser drawer in the guest room.

Last fall I read one. I found it on the desk in the upstairs hall, and wondered if, with Grandpa dead, she

reread the letters, maybe one a night. I sat down on the top stair and read it quickly.

It was summer, 1931. Grandma was twenty-two. She was living at her family home in Wilkinsburg; Grandpa was with his family in Keene, New Hampshire. She wrote the letter at nearly midnight, after she and her sister had returned home from a party.

Grandma once showed me one of her party dresses from back then; ankle-length midnight-blue lace in a spiderweb pattern over a silk shift of deep burgundy. I imagined her in that, her hair gleaming, her face smooth and pale and delicate, her beautiful script flowing from her fountain pen onto the page.

She told him about the party, who had been there, what they had eaten, the new record the host had and how they had all laughed as they danced to it. Then she told him about coming home and standing on the back porch as her sister went on up to bed; standing there and looking north, up at the black sky and the brilliant stars that glittered across it. How quiet the night was.

Perhaps she was thinking of him as she stood on that porch, gazing northward. But I wonder if she thought not of him, of how marrying him would cast her onto one path for the rest of her life, but of what could be. She was college-educated and pretty, strong-willed and intelligent. If she didn't marry that tall, slow-speaking Yankee, what other possibilities might there be for her?

Of course, young women back then were supposed to marry and raise a family. But Grandma's mother went off to claim land in Nebraska before she settled down, finally marrying when she was almost thirty; and Grandma was twenty-five and a teacher when she married Grandpa. What had she given up, besides her job, when she married Grandpa? What had she dreamed of when she stood on that porch, the nighttime sky spread above her, the hem of her lace dress brushing her ankles?

If I ask her, I know she'll tell me she was thinking of Grandpa. And maybe after all these years she believes that. I don't. I have to believe that within her a freer spirit dreamed of bursting the bonds of convention. I have to believe there is more to her than her stately house, her life devoted to it and her husband and her child. I have to believe there will be more than that for me.

A couple of days after I buy the cigarettes, Kris and I go to the pool again. As we walk along the concrete edge, I look around at the other teenagers, hoping to see someone I know. I do. The shoplifter, Diane, is on the other side, wearing a bikini that's more string than fabric. She's sitting between the legs of a dark-haired boy, rubbing her shoulders and back against his bare chest. Barbara and Cheryl are there too, and a few other kids. Diane seems to be looking my way, and I wave. She squints, then after a pause nods back at me.

Kris and I don't talk. We lie on our towels and read. Unnerved by silence, I feel I should make polite conversation. But he doesn't seem to care to speak to me, so I tell myself not to care either.

After about half an hour, we both decide to swim. I ease into the water, for the one thing they haven't been able to teach me at the Y was how to dive. Kris can dive, and he turns smoothly underwater to swim back to me. He's like a

53

fish, his body spearing through the water, arms and legs rhythmic and fluid. We tread water, swimming a little this way, a little that way, dodging rambunctious kids and getting splashed when a boy cannonballs into the pool.

"Can you swim underwater?" Kris asks.

"Yes."

"You want to see who can swim the farthest?"

"Sure."

We slip under the water and head for the shallow end. His long legs perfectly suited to the frog kick, he easily moves ahead of me. Even after I've surfaced for air he's still going, steadily, tirelessly, slipping past the watchful mothers and shrieking children like a magical sea creature no one else can see. When he reaches the wall and stands, pushing his hair back, he turns and looks for me. I wave and breaststroke toward him, some of my animosity sliding off me. The only other person I know who can swim like that is my brother.

"You won," I say when I reach him. "I'm much better on top of the water."

He takes a deep breath. "You want to race? The length of the pool, freestyle?"

"You're on."

We crouch at the wall at the shallow end, arms out in front, feet braced to push off.

"Ready, set, go!"

With a great splash we start. He pulls in front quickly, and I drive hard to catch up. Halfway there he's barely a body length ahead of me, but my lungs are burning. When I snag a breath every third stroke, I don't get enough air. My legs weakening, my shoulders barely strong enough to lift my leaden arms, but I push on. I'm beside him now. I think he's slowing. Just a little faster, a little harder . . .

My hand slams against the concrete wall and I nearly knock my head on it too. I grab hold, gasping, and look for Kris. He's holding on, too, breathing just as hard.

"Who won?" I ask. My voice is faint.

"You did." He takes one more deep breath, then tries to breathe regularly. "I saw you touch just before I did. You're a good swimmer."

I feel as if my body won't move again for three or four days, but nod and say, "Thanks."

We glide over to the stairs and I pull myself up them. Not only are my arms and legs weak, but an ominous fluttering has crept into my stomach. I walk warily, as if a knife is poised to slice through me, and sprawl on my towel. A great shudder rolls over me and the fluttering worsens to a frightening cramp, like a great fist closing around me. I roll onto my side, hands covering my stomach.

"What's wrong?" Kris asks.

"Cramps," I mutter. I'm cold and shivering. The shivering hurts, too, but I don't want to move to pull my towel around me.

"Cramps? Are you getting your period?"

I open my eyes, frowning at him.

"I've got sisters, Ginnie. I know what happens to girls every month."

"No, it's not my period. I must have—" A solid punch hits my stomach. "Must have pulled a muscle," I gasp.

"Oh. You shouldn't have swum so hard. What can I do?"

His hand is on my shoulder, and I concentrate on the

55

feel of it, turning my mind away from the pain. It doesn't work.

"I don't know." Tears and moans well up inside me. Menstrual cramps were never this bad.

"Is she all right?" a voice above me says.

"She thinks she pulled a muscle. But it shouldn't hurt like this."

Trembling and sweaty, I clutch myself, curling into a ball. Pain radiates up into my breasts and down to my thighs.

"Ginnie." The person standing over me stoops down. It's Diane. "Can we do anything?"

I shake my head, and that little movement does me in. "Oh God," I mutter. "I'm gonna be sick."

"It's okay," Diane says calmly, helping me up. "We'll walk over to the locker room, okay? Slow and easy. You're not going to get sick. Come on. That's good. You can make it."

People whisper as we slowly make our way to the other end of the pool. I hear one little boy say, "What's wrong with her, Mommy?"

Diane helps me over the wooden plank that separates the concrete around the pool from the concrete inside the locker room. Leading me to an end stall, she lifts the seat and squats me down. I grip the sides of the bowl, bending over it, and a painful force rips up through my body. I vomit, but my stomach is nearly empty. Bile comes up, and then it's dry heaves. The cramping forces me to retch again and again, until I'm exhausted.

"You okay?" Diane asks when I ease down onto the cold floor.

I nod, amazed that I do feel better. My muscles are

sore, but the cramping seems to have ended. Cautiously, I stand up and look at her. "What happened?"

She shakes her head as she walks me to a sink, saying she watched me race, then saw me collapse on my towel and figured something was wrong. She grins as she turns on the water. "If I swam that far that fast, I'd probably collapse too. Maybe you did just pull a muscle."

I rinse my mouth and straighten. My stomach protests, but the violent cramping doesn't start again.

Outside, Kris gazes anxiously at me. He reaches out one hand, but doesn't touch me. "Did you throw up?"

"Not too much."

The three of us walk slowly back to the towels, and Diane stands over me as I sit down. "This probably isn't exactly a good time to talk about it," she says, "but I thought you'd like to get together sometime."

I nod. "My grandmother's name is Charlotte Alcott. She's in the phone book."

"I'll look you up. Hope you feel better."

I sort of smile. "Can't feel worse. And hey, Diane. Thanks."

She shrugs. "No problem." Her smile flashes. "I hope you don't have to do the same for me sometime."

She leaves and I lie down. Kris bends over me, one hand raised again as if to touch me. The urge to touch him, too, swirls vaguely through me, a desire for comfort after the pain. My eyes are closing with exhaustion, though. I manage to lift a hand and brush it against his. He says something, but I'm already asleep.

S E V E N

July 5

Dear Ginnie,
   Early, early Wednesday morning. Your father's still asleep. We went out to dinner with the Waverlys last night and didn't get in until late. Your father said when we got home that he thinks he might be too old for such a wild night life.

   I haven't heard from Tom this week. I guess they're deep in the Maine wilderness, up the Allagash. Remember how, the first year he went to the camp, we kept track on a map of where he would be each day?

   I'm not sure what I'll do today. Maybe I'll drive to Brandywine, check out the British soldier in the dungeon. Or go into the city and spend the afternoon at the art museum. Or I could go to a matinee. Now that's real decadence. Too bad your father has to work.

I was glad to talk to you on Sunday. You sound good, though maybe a little lonely. But at least you and Kris got together. I always thought he was a nice boy.

Speaking of boys, have you heard from Denny? Does he miss you? You didn't mention him either in your letter or on the phone, so I'm wondering if you're missing him?

No new gossip on the street. I think it's too hot for anyone to do anything. I hear your father getting up, so I'll sign off for now and ask him if he has anything to add.

Love,
Mom

Ginnie—just a quick note before I dash off to work. Everything's fine here, though we miss you. Hope you're having a good time with Grandma. Sorry I missed talking to you on Sunday. Your mother had told me she was calling you at four, but when I got home from playing golf at 3:30 she said she'd already talked to you.

No matter. I'll make sure we talk this weekend.

Love you,
Dad

July 8

Dear Mom and Dad,

Something weird happened when I went to the pool with Kris yesterday. He and I were racing the length of the pool— he's a real good swimmer—and I won, but then I got these horrible cramps and was sick to my stomach. A girl I met a couple of days before was there, and she and Kris helped me. The pain went away after I was sick. I suppose I just pulled a muscle.

Kris is an okay guy. He's very smart and doesn't seem interested in much outside of books. When we went to the pool the other day, he was reading Thoreau's Walden. *He's even graduating from high school a year early. I don't think we have a lot in common.*

Not much else is going on here. Sounds like you're doing okay back there in Philadelphia.

I sign the letter and stuff it into an envelope. Grandma has written a couple of letters, too, and I take them with me to the mailbox across the street, on the corner below the Webers'. As I walk over, I wonder if Kris sees me, but then remember he's working with his older brother that day, helping him take care of other people's lawns and gardens.

I drop the letters in the box, then wait to cross back as a bus roars up the hill. Its diesel fumes sweep over me, and I hold my breath and close my eyes.

When I open them again, I'm looking right at Grandma's house, white bricks gleaming, green-and-white-striped awnings shading the porch and front windows of the dining room and upstairs bedrooms. I know the house has looked like that for thirty years, and wonder if my home in Philadelphia will look the same when I'm grown up. Will I bring my children back and watch them race in the front door to greet their grandma and grandpa?

This foreign image of myself with children, my parents thin and gray, hits me wrong. I run it through my mind again—imagining myself pulling into the driveway, my mother opening the front door and stepping down onto the tiny concrete porch, my son or daughter bolting from the car and into her arms—yet it is still unbelievable.

I've fantasized about getting married for years. When I had nightmares as a child and was too afraid to go back to sleep, Mom would tell me to think about horses or getting married, so the happy thoughts would chase the bad ones away. I've imagined my wedding dozens of times, certain of its eventual reality, certain of life continuing in a pattern established generations ago.

A different reality intrudes, though. The reality of my mother saying marriages have to go someplace, implying hers and Dad's isn't going anywhere. The reality of my mother sleeping on the couch because—she said—of the heat. The reality of my dad thinking of getting an evening job again, even though the reason they shipped me off to Pittsburgh was so they could be alone together. The reality of last summer, when it was just Dad and me after I got home from camp, and Dad went out nearly every night, not coming back until after ten. I didn't know where he went, or with whom. I didn't want to know. Didn't want to know what he meant when he said, "Maybe someday I'll explain to you."

Several cars passed while I stood beside the mailbox, staring at Grandma's house. As I start across the street, I wonder what my parents are really doing in Philadelphia.

Kris comes over late that afternoon to ask me to a movie. I don't want to go anywhere with him. Getting sick in front of someone fosters an awkward intimacy, and I'm uneasy sharing that with him. But since he comes to our front door and I speak to him through the screen while Grandma sits in her chair listening, I can't say no. I ask what movie, and he says *The Silence of the Lambs*.

61

I've seen it, but I say all right.

He tells me he was thinking of going to the seven-thirty showing that night, but his mom needs the car. Would I mind walking?

It's farther to the theater than to the pool. I say, "Wait a minute," and walk across the room to Grandma.

"Grandma," I say, kneeling on the floor by her chair, "is it all right if I take the car tonight? The movie doesn't start until nearly eight, so it'll be way after ten by the time it's over. That's awfully late to be walking home."

"Oh, of course," she says. "Why don't you ask Kris in for some lemonade?"

Because I don't want to. I walk back to the door. "It's okay. I can use our car. What time should we go?"

He shrugs. "Quarter to seven?"

"Okay." As he turns away I ask if he'd like some lemonade.

"No thanks," he says. "I'll be over at six forty-five."

He is. Exactly. I don't bother letting him in, but step outside and lead him down the driveway to the garage. He helps me open the door, and Grandpa's car gleams in the dim interior.

It is white, wide, and sleek, with narrow running boards along the sides and small fins rising in the back. The front windshield is high and domed; the back window is small and slopes in an elegant curve down to the trunk. The green interior still smells new.

Even when he first bought it, Grandpa didn't drive the car much—he and Grandma weren't travelers. It made two trips over the mountains to Philadelphia, then

Grandpa had a stroke and no longer drove long distances. He would take Grandma to church and shopping, but not much else. The car spent most of its time in the garage and is still unscratched and undented.

Since it was built before seat belts and emergency flashers became mandatory, the car has neither. It doesn't have a gearshift either. Instead, black buttons marked Park and Drive and so on are lined vertically on the far left side of the dashboard.

The car starts easily. I let it warm up before pressing Reverse and backing out onto the drive. Kris shuts the garage door, then gets in beside me. He searches for a seat belt, irritating me.

I continue backing down the drive. The bushes scrape familiarly along the sides of the car, and I run up onto the low curb only once. I hope Kris doesn't notice.

At the street, I check for cars, even though between the blind spots in the Dodge and the neighbor's tree I can't see a thing, and spin out onto the street. I head the car down the hill, punch Drive, and take off. Kris's head jerks back against the seat.

"Do you know where you're going?" he asks.

"Yup."

By car, the theater is only a short trip away. I happily careen into the parking lot, the big white Dodge dwarfing the little imported Japanese cars. As I slide into a parking space, I wonder if I've made Kris nervous, but he seems calm.

We have to stand in line. The weather is once more hot and humid, and with the front of the theater facing southwest, the setting sun hits fully on us.

"God, it's hot," I say.

Kris, his arms folded across his chest, glances at me. "You shouldn't have worn long pants."

He is wearing shorts, long cotton shorts that cover his skinny thighs halfway to his knees. Turning away from him, I hope the other kids in line don't think he's my boyfriend.

Does Denny ever feel like this, I wonder, embarrassed at being seen with a too tall, too thin, too brainy-looking girl?

I enjoy *The Silence of the Lambs* the second time. Kris likes it too. As we leave the theater he looks at his watch, then tells me it's late.

"I told my grandmother I wouldn't be home until after ten," I say, unlocking the car. "Do you want to go someplace?"

He looks startled. Does he think I'm suggesting we go parking? Forget it. I just don't want to go home yet.

We get in the car and he doesn't speak for a minute. At last, he says, "There's a Denny's not too far from here." He glances at me. "Isn't that your boyfriend's name?"

"Yeah. Let's go there."

There are a lot of teenagers in Denny's. No families this late at night. We're led to a table by the windows. I order chocolate ice cream and Kris asks for a sundae. While we wait, I light a cigarette and stare at my reflection in the window. This imperfect mirror softens my square jaw and big nose, and makes my eyes look deep and mysterious. I admire the way I smoke, elegantly lifting the cigarette to my lips, then letting it dangle between my long fingers as I tilt my head up to blow smoke at the—

"Hey, Ginnie."

64

Startled from my vanity, I spin around. Diane is standing beside our table. She looks the same as when I first saw her, her hair a curly mass, her eyes made bigger and bluer by heavy eye shadow and dark liner, her jeans tight across her hips and flat stomach. Her top is black again, a slinky, silky fabric. She stands with her hands on her hips, and I can see that she has red polish on her nails, but most of it's scraped off, leaving only ragged circles of color.

The same guy who was with her at the pool stands beside her, tall and tough-looking. Like Denny but not as cute.

"Hey, Diane," I say. "What's going on?"

"Not much." She introduces her boyfriend as Larry, then glances around the restaurant. "This place is dead. What are you up to?"

I make a small gesture toward Kris. "We went to see *The Silence of the Lambs.*"

"Yeah?" Larry says. "Isn't that a great movie? Did you catch that scene where that doctor tears off that cop's face and then, like, wears it?"

I nod. "What are you guys up to?"

"We thought we'd go cruising," Diane says. "Barbara and her boyfriend Joe are here." She waves behind her. "And a couple of other kids. You want to come?"

I ignore the way Kris is staring at me. "Sure."

"Ginnie," Kris says. "We haven't gotten our ice cream yet."

I give Diane a look that says, Isn't this guy a drag? "We can cancel the order."

He's about to argue when our waitress returns, slipping past Larry to set our ice cream down on the table. Kris's expression is irritatingly triumphant.

65

"Hey, we can wait," Diane says. "We're right over there. Come on over when you're done."

Diane and Larry saunter away, hands in each other's back pockets. A fierce desire to be with Denny washes over me. I imagine I can feel his arm around my shoulders, his hand drifting down toward my breast. I glare at Kris.

"You don't have to come," I say, digging my spoon into the dark ice cream.

"I'll come. You might get lost. But don't you think you should call your grandmother?"

I stare at him, then shake my head. "God, you're hopeless."

I finish my ice cream and ask for the check as Kris slowly, deliberately savors each tiny spoonful of his sundae. I'm afraid Diane and her friends will get bored and leave, but they don't.

At last Kris is through. We split the tip, then I give him my part of the bill and he goes to the cash register to pay. I walk over to Diane's table.

There are seven of them, and Diane introduces me. Along with Barbara and Joe are two other guys—Phil, who has long blond hair, and Steve, dark-haired, good-looking, and older—and a girl named Debbie. Debbie doesn't seem to be with either of the guys, but she's sitting very close to Steve.

"You ready?" Diane asks as Kris walks over to me.

I nod.

"Let's go," Larry says.

They stand as one, shoving their chairs back. We head for the door and out into the hot night.

E I G H T

Narrow and dark, the road curves dangerously through thick woods. It dips and bends, hiding cars until they're nearly upon us, their headlights glaring in my face for an instant, freezing me, then sweeping past.

Kris has no idea where we are. He lost his sense of direction two turns back. I'm not worried about that, only about keeping the big Dodge within the boundaries of the road. At this speed, the steering wheel is prey to some force I learned about in physics class and tugs to the right, urging us toward the trees. I struggle to tame the wheel, not jerking the car but easing it over and around the hills and curves. And I try to keep the taillights of Steve's car in sight.

I'm scared, my hands paralyzed around the steering

wheel, my right leg rigid and aching from my foot lying heavy on the gas pedal. I don't tell Kris, though. He's scared too. Our cruising began as cruising with Denny always did, a slow traversing of the main drag through the neighborhood, racing yellow lights and checking out the other cars. When Larry and Diane, followed by Joe and Barbara, then Steve and Phil and Debbie, turned off onto a residential road that rose straight up the side of a hill, I was surprised but not worried. Perhaps we were going to a friend's house.

Then Larry turned off onto another road, and another, and another, each darker and wilder than the last. There are no lights to show anyone lives along here. I imagine that an accident would be fatal, if only because it would be hours before you could get to a hospital.

Visions of all the things that could happen to us clutter the part of my mind that isn't intent on driving. Haunted houses and psychotic killers and sadistic small-town sheriffs dance in front of me, almost less frightening than the image of the Dodge spinning out of control and flying into an oak tree.

"Let's go back, Ginnie," Kris says.

I don't look at him, just as I don't look at the speedometer. "You said you don't know where we are."

"If we follow this road back, I'm sure I could figure out where to go. Or we could probably find someone to ask."

The psychotic killer lifts a glistening knife. "Well, where do you suggest I turn around, Kris? This car's a little big to hang a U-turn right in the middle of the road."

"If we look for one, I'm sure we'll see a turnoff."

I know he is right. We should stop. Someone could get

68

hurt. The car could be smashed. But a part of me thrives on this challenge. Even now I'm getting better at driving, anticipating dips and bumps and bends and sliding through them, no nervous twitching of the wheel. I'm even getting used to the speed, and wonder if I can push it a little higher. That might get me too close to Steve, though.

I realize abruptly I'm too close now and ease up on the accelerator. Steve is slowing down. What happened? Was there an accident? No, we would have heard something. Did he lose the others? How could he lose them? There is nowhere to go but straight on.

He slows to a crawl and on a long straightaway, where we can be seen by cars coming from either direction, he pulls as far off the road as he can and stops. His flashers blink on.

"You should put your flashers on too," Kris says as I push Park and set the emergency brake.

"I don't have any," I say, but I flick the right blinker on.

We get out and walk toward Steve's car. His door is open and he has one leg out. We can hear Debbie screaming something at him; then he steps out onto the road and slams the door shut.

"They're crazy," he says to us, jerking his thumb down the road, where Larry's and Joe's cars have disappeared. "They were going to get us killed. They may still kill themselves."

I say nothing. Steve has done the right thing. The same thing Kris wanted me to do. The challenge, the thrilling test of my skill, had begun to intoxicate me, and my desire to keep on driving is stupid and dangerous next to their desire to keep on living.

The passenger door on Steve's car slams shut, and Debbie stalks over to us, her long straight hair swinging viciously around her shoulders.

"You jerk!" she yells in Steve's face. "Are you an idiot? What the hell did you stop for?"

"What do you think I stopped for?" Steve shouts back. "I have this strange urge to live until I'm at least nineteen!"

"God, I can't believe this." She stares down the road, but there's nothing to see. "They're probably all laughing their heads off at us." She glares at Steve again, but since she's nearly a foot shorter than he, she's not particularly intimidating. "I can't believe I ever wanted to date you."

Steve seems surprised she was interested in him, and I don't understand why. He's tall and attractive, though maybe his chin's weak. A lot of girls must be after him. A nice, sensible guy too. Grandma would love him.

We all get back into our cars. Steve easily makes the U-turn in his Toyota; I have to back up once to avoid going off the road. He drives slowly, leading us back. It's a long way. When we reach the street Kris and my grandmother live on, I flash my brights at him and turn on my blinker. He beeps in answer. I speed up the hill, taking the turn into the driveway too fast and jostling Kris and myself. I stop in front of the garage for him to open the door, then I careful drive the big car in.

When I get out, I see Kris has followed me inside the garage.

"Um . . ." he says. "I had a nice time, Ginnie. Do you

suppose we could go out some other night?"

"Sure," I say quickly, anxious to get into the house. Although it's after midnight, I'm sure I saw the silhouette of my grandmother in one of the living-room windows. I imagine she's at the back door, wondering what Kris and I are doing in the garage.

"I have to go," I say.

He steps toward me as I try to slip past him. His hand brushes my arm, and I stop.

"Can I kiss you good night?" he asks.

Surprised, I don't answer for a moment. I don't really want to kiss him, but my curiosity urges me to. "Okay."

It's dark in the garage, and when he leans down, he misses. His lips touch the high left corner of my mouth. He pulls back quickly.

"Here," I say. I put my hands on his face and bring his head down.

Our lips touch. His are dry and tight. He presses them against mine, and I almost open my mouth to him, because that's what I would do for Denny. But he's not Denny. I step away and bump into the car. Kris stands still for a moment, then turns.

"Good night," he calls as he walks out of the garage.

Grandma decides I need more punishment the next day. She treated me to the "I was so worried about you and you were too inconsiderate to call" routine the night before, and this morning it's sad and stern stares across the dining-room table. She sips her coffee while I eat my Sunday breakfast of eggs and coffee cake, wishing I had something to read. Reading is not allowed at the table, but it would be better than catching her frowns.

After breakfast I atone for my sins by washing all the downstairs windows and mirrors. That loosens Grandma up, and she chatters away during our lunch of deviled ham on thin white bread.

I'm finishing my milk when she says, "Your mother called last night."

"She did? Why didn't you tell me?" No answer. Right. I was being punished. "What did she say?"

"Oh, not much. Only that it was hot and she missed you."

"I guess she'll just call today as usual."

"I'm sure she will," Grandma says positively.

Standing abruptly, she carries her plate and glass to the kitchen. I hear her rinsing them, then she returns to the dining room. She seems about to speak when the phone rings. She walks out to the living room to answer it.

"Hel-lo-o?" she says. "Oh, hello, Kay. How *are* you? How was the operation?"

She's obviously settling in for a long chat. I take my own dishes out to the kitchen, rinse them, and leave them in the sink. What to do now? I could go to the pool or Burger King, which is all that would be open on a Sunday. But Diane might be at either place. Debbie was probably right last night; those other kids laughed when they realized we'd chickened out. I'm glad I got home in one piece, but I'm not eager to hear that laughter directly in my face.

What to do?

I go to the pool. I don't see anyone I know, and choose a barren area to spread out my towel. Not interested in socializing, or even in swimming, I immerse myself in *Dragonquest*, one of the books in Anne McCaffrey's fantasy series. I am Lessa, riding the great golden dragon Ramoth, when someone's wet feet plop onto the edge of my towel, and droplets of water dot the page.

Angry at the interruption, I scowl up at the person. The sun is behind her, haloing around her head, and I don't recognize her.

"Hi, Ginnie," she says.

Can't place the voice either. "Hi."

"I heard you were out with Diane last night."

"You know, you're standing right in the sun and it's real hard looking up at you like this."

"Oh. Sorry." She quickly sits down on the grass beside me and smiles. "That better?"

"Sure." I recognize her now. Cheryl, Diane's other friend from the shoplifting escapade. "Yeah, I was with Diane last night."

"Did you hear what happened to her and Barb?"

I shake my head as a sensation of dread envelopes me. My own ghastly vision of what could happen on that road reappears. Oh God, I think, don't let them be dead.

"They're both grounded," Cheryl says, sounding oddly triumphant.

"What happened?"

"You know they were out joyriding." She looks to me for confirmation. I shrug. "Well, along comes a cop and before you know it they're all down at the jail charged with reckless driving. I guess Mrs. LaSalle—that's Diane's mom—and Mrs. Myrtle—Barb's mother—were pretty angry at Diane and Barb, and they've both been grounded for a month! And they're never allowed to see Larry or Joe again. God." Cheryl shakes her head. "Diane must be so upset. She really loves Larry."

I stare at the pool, at the jumping, shrieking kids, and silently thank Steve. We could have been arrested too. Being caught doing something dumb is somehow worse than being hurt or killed while you're doing it. At least if you're dead no one can tell you how stupid you were.

"Well," I say, "that's too bad for Diane and Barbara."

"I'll say! Diane's not allowed out of the house at all for two weeks, then she's only allowed out during the day for two more weeks. She's not allowed to stay on the phone for more than ten minutes at a time. And of course she can't smoke. She's probably having a nicotine fit right now."

I study Cheryl out of the corner of my eye. Her voice is light, nearly gleeful, as though she relishes Diane's misfortune. I puzzle it through, remembering an English teacher's explanation of dramatic tragedy. A tragedy makes us feel better, for no matter how bad our own lives are, someone else's is worse.

I glance again at Cheryl. Diane is pretty and thin. Barbara, with that black hair and those ice-green eyes, is striking. Cheryl is dumpy and plain. But at least she stayed out of trouble. She isn't grounded for a month. I pick up my cigarettes and offer her one. There is justice in this world.

The phone rings after dinner that night. I'm washing dishes, so Grandma answers it.

"Ginnie," she calls. "It's for you."

I dry my hands as I walk into the living room. I doubt it's Kris. He'd just walk across the street. And if it were my mother—who still hasn't called—Grandma would be chatting with her. I pick up the phone and turn toward the window, away from her.

"Hello?"

"Hey, Ginnie. It's Diane."

"Hey." Oh, great. Grandma's going to love this. "How's it going?"

"Are you kidding? It sucks. Did you hear what happened?"

"Cheryl told me."

"Oh yeah. She knows the whole story. My mother called her mother first thing this morning, and went on talking for a half hour, complaining about what a disappointment I am, how bad I'm turning out to be, blah, blah, blah. Christ, don't you just hate mothers?"

I try to agree, but somehow a "yes" can't force its way up my throat.

Diane goes on. "Now my dad, he's cool about it. He just says he's glad I didn't get hurt. And he pointed out to my mom that Larry was driving, not me. What could I do?"

I imagine she didn't want to do anything, but still I think of Debbie screaming at Steve when he stopped. The driver does have the final say.

"So Dad's cool. He thinks I should only be grounded for two weeks. And maybe see Larry again after a month or so. But shit. Guess who runs this house? Mom says jump and we all say how high. She . . ."

75

There's a pause, then Diane mutters, "Christ. She's standing at the door to my bedroom, pointing at her watch and telling me I've got to get off the phone. Listen, maybe you could come over tomorrow. I'm not allowed to leave the yard—makes me sound like some damn dog—but I can have friends over. Maybe you could come."

"Maybe."

"Hey, what happened to you guys last night? Joe told us he didn't see yours or Steve's headlights for a while before the cops ran us down."

"It was getting late," I say blandly. "I had to get home. My grandmother, you know."

"Yeah. Tell me about it. All right!" she yells away from the phone. "I'm hanging up, okay? Get off my back! Gotta go, Ginnie. I'll call you tomorrow."

"Grea—" She's already hung up. I hang up too, and glance at Grandma.

"Who was that, dear?"

"A girl named Diane. Kris and I met her and some of her friends at the pool that day he and I went there. We met up with them again at the movie last night. That's why I was so late."

"I see," Grandma says. "What's her last name?"

"LaSalle."

"That's French. I don't believe I know any LaSalles. Where does she live?"

"I don't know, Grandma. I've only met her twice."

"Well, my goodness." She laughs. "You could have asked. People do that when they meet, you know."

"What difference would it make? I wouldn't know if she came from a good neighborhood or not. Will you not

76

let me see her if you don't approve of where she lives?"

"Oh!" She turns her head away. Her lips tighten and she tries to straighten her crooked back. "That is an unkind accusation, Ginnie."

She looks so proud yet injured, I almost take it back. But I want to fight. My whole body tingles, as if the frustration within me—the frustration at having no control anywhere in my life—has exploded, its shards scraping against my insides. I won't let Grandma off the hook. She does judge people by their family and home.

"Well, what difference does it make," I ask in a loud voice, "where Diane is from? Bad people can come from so-called good neighborhoods and vice versa."

"True," she says. "But a person's roots will always tell true in the end. When you're older you'll understand what I mean."

When you're older. "Who cares about when I'm older?" I yell. "I'm this age now. Why does everyone treat me as though I'm not worth talking to until I'm twenty-one?"

Distress wrinkles Grandma's smooth brow. "That's silly. We talk to you now. You're very mature for your age."

I stomp across the room, then swing back around. "So what's *really* going on with Mom and Dad? What did she mean when she said they didn't know where their marriage was going? What's wrong with it?"

I've shocked myself as much as her. She holds my gaze for a moment, her childlike blue eyes wide and bewildered, then she pushes herself up out of her chair. "You'll have to ask your mother," she says quietly, and walks from the room.

I plunk down on the bottom stair. What *is* going on with Mom and Dad? Why didn't they say anything before, when I was there, and not right before they sent me away? Why did they hide it?

My friends say I'm crazy when I tell them my parents never fight. Their own homes reverberate with their parents' raised voices. Your parents have to fight, they say. I shrug and answer, If they do, I never hear them.

I've always assumed they like their calm, relaxed marriage. I like it. When I'm at my friends' and hear their parents going at it, or even worse, when my friends fight with their mothers or fathers, I cringe in embarrassment and confusion. I wonder how these people can live together, can say they love each other when they're always angry at each other. I don't know what my parents would do if I screamed at them, and I'm not going to find out.

I stay on the bottom step, gazing out the window on the other side of the living room, watching the world darken within its small squares. Philadelphia is far away. Farther than I thought.

N I N E

The mail comes early to Grandma's, before ten o'clock. She always greets Bill, the mailman, and they exchange Hello's and How are you's and Looks like a nice or not so nice day. Monday morning, the morning after our argument, the morning after my mother doesn't call, Bill brings a letter for me. I am slouched on the couch and hear him say, "I've got one for your granddaughter today."

I sit up. In the two weeks I've been there, I've gotten two letters from my mother and one from my best friend, Karen. None from Denny. I walk to the door, and Bill hands me the small white envelope.

The handwriting is Denny's, heavy and cramped. Ugly even. I don't care. Clutching it in one hand, I drift out the back door and down to the garden. I perch on a big stone by the climbing rose and carefully tear open the envelope.

The letter is short. He still loves me, but I'm not there and he's lonely. He's been dating. When I come back maybe we can get together again, though he really likes this girl. He's really sorry, but what could he do?

Love, Denny.

I read it three times, as if I keep missing something. But that's all there is. It's as easy and quick as that. My eyes unfocused, my mind blank, I crumple the letter and hurl it across the garden. The faint breeze defeats it, dropping it quickly to the ground. I stare at it, concentrating on the angles and creases I've crushed into it, the bits of black writing that edge up one side; concentrating on it and not the feelings threatening to rip through me.

The paper's whiteness glares against the bright green grass, offending me, the garden. I get up and kick it. It arcs nicely and lands in front of the snapdragons, their stalks, heavy with blossoms, majestic above it.

"I don't care," I tell the snapdragons. "I can be as aloof as you. I never loved him. I—"

I never needed him, is what I want to say, but the breath is knocked out of me by the memory of his James Dean smile when I'd run out of the house and swing up behind him on his motorcycle. I needed him looking at me, seeing me, wanting to be with me.

The letter is blurring at the angled edges. The writing seems to drip into the ground. His smile turns sly. I've seen it before. It's how he smiled at Michelle, large-breasted, blond Michelle, at the party last summer.

Michelle. Oh God, not her.

I drop down hard onto the grass, hang my head between my knees, and cry.

Grandma comes to find me. She's beside me before I hear her, and I lift my head as she strokes my hair.

"Was it a letter from Denny?" she asks.

I nod, not looking at her. Tears still sting my eyes. My throat is tight and raw.

"Come inside. I'll make you some tea."

I sit on the high stool in the kitchen as she fills the kettle and puts it on the fire. She plucks two tea bags from the box, then turns to me.

"Why don't you pick some nice teacups from the china closet?"

I slide off the stool and walk into the dining room. Grandma would never drink from a big, hefty pottery mug, only delicate china cups. She has nearly two dozen, all different. Someday, she tells me, they'll be mine.

I choose a fluted turquoise one for her, then hesitate over mine. Most of them are flowery, and I don't want that. At last I pull from the back a simple cup, small and mint green, a design in gold at the rim and a gold handle. I turn it over. Royal Albert. Bone China. England.

Wouldn't Denny laugh to see me drinking out of this? I swaggered when I was with him, but still I like the feel of delicate china.

Grandma has poured the boiling water into the teapot. "There's some Scottish shortbread in the cupboard," she says as she slices a lemon into thin wedges. "Way in the back. Why don't you get it?"

Shortbread at eleven in the morning? Obviously, rules are suspended when your boyfriend breaks up with you. I rummage around in the cupboard and find the unopened package of shortbread. As she arranges the lemon slices in a cut-glass dish, I lay out the thick fingers of shortbread on a decorated plate. We're ready for tea, and she leads the way to the living room.

The preparation and ceremony have dulled the pain for the moment. I think of nothing as Grandma pours the tea, then focus on my fingers squeezing lemon into my cup and stirring with a small silver spoon. I move slowly, so I don't jar loose even a fragment of hurt, the tiniest memory of how he looked in the moonlit woods, lying on top of me, whispering that he lov—

"When I was about your age," Grandma says, "I fell in love for the first time."

I nod. I've heard the story about her and Grandpa.

"His name was Charles, and he had the most beautiful blue eyes I've ever seen."

My head snaps up. Grandpa's name wasn't Charles and he didn't have blue eyes. They were brown, like my mother's.

Grandma sighs. "We were so young. I was just eighteen and he was twenty-two, and we . . . I wonder where he is now."

Grandma loved someone other than Grandpa? How come no one ever told me this?

"How'd you meet him?" I ask, nibbling on a piece of shortbread.

"Oh." She laughs her little laugh. "I had gone out with some friends, and one of them knew him. We were walking to a shop to have tea. I remember it was a bitterly cold day. He didn't seem to mind the cold. He was smartly dressed, and when we turned a corner the wind blew his hat off. He ran after it so quick, he caught it before it went ten feet."

"Did he have tea with you?" I ask.

"Oh, yes. We thought it was rather dashing to have this handsome man at our table. He was quite charming, and he had the nicest smile."

She stares vaguely across the room, as if she sees again that handsome man with the beautiful blue eyes. But I am frustrated by her words. She is talking like an old lady. "He had the nicest smile." I don't believe she was thinking that on that winter day almost seventy years ago. Surely she hasn't always been so stiff, so conscientiously superficial.

"Did you flirt with him?" I ask, goading her.

She is offended. She turns her head toward me, her smile fading. "When I was your age, young ladies did not *flirt* with gentlemen."

"Then what did you *do*?"

"We talked. We got to know one another."

"That's it?"

"Well, we certainly didn't hop into bed with each other, the way your generation does."

"Speak for yourself," I mutter. But I can be happy about one thing. I didn't have sex with Denny. He can get it from Michelle now.

I try to be tough about that, but the pain is savage. He'll regret it, I tell myself, but I don't believe myself.

Grandma still looks offended and proper, her teacup in

one hand as she delicately eats shortbread. Does she think I slept with Denny? I want to tell her I didn't, but that sort of honesty isn't encouraged in my family.

"The shortbread is good," I tell her instead.

She sighs and smiles. "You'll have other disappointments in your life, Ginnie, but you'll forget all about them when you truly fall in love."

Romantic mush, I think. Like Mom telling me to think about my wedding after I scream myself awake from a nightmare. But maybe those little fantasies are okay if you know they're just for chasing away ghosts.

I sit back, sipping my tea, and tell myself that Grandma is right. One day I'll fall in love, and Denny and all the other men I knew won't matter. Just like Charles doesn't matter to her anymore.

T E N

"Do you know anything about Charles?" I ask Mom when she finally calls that night. I'm in the living room and Grandma is in the kitchen, so I keep my voice down. Her eyesight might be fading, but her hearing is sharper than anyone's.

"Charles who?" Mom asks.

"The Charles Grandma knew before she met Grandpa."

Mom is silent for a moment. I hear her draw in a lungful of cigarette smoke, then let it out. "I guess she told me about him once, but I really can't remember."

"Oh. Well, how ya doin'?"

"Ginnie, I have to talk to you. It's about . . . it's about your father and I."

"Me. My father and me. You can never get your pronouns straight, Mom."

"All right, Ginnie. Would you just listen?"

I say nothing, sinking into the couch cushion, and she goes on.

"As I told you, your father and I wanted some time alone together to work through a few . . . problems. I know you can't understand what it's like, but . . . Well, people never stop growing and changing. Actually, I suppose some people do; they just stagnate someplace. But people like your father and me, we're continually growing, continually wanting different things from life. It's like right now, your goal is to go to college. But in four years that will be over, and your next goal will be a job. And probably marriage . . ."

Don't count on it, I think, my hand clenching around the phone. I slip off my sandals and pull my legs up to sit cross-legged. The soles of my feet are filthy.

"So," she continues, "I have new goals now. Not that I'll ever stop being your mother, but you and Tom are almost all grown up, and I need something more in my life."

"Are you leaving?" My throat is too tight, but I squeeze the words out.

"Of course I'm not leaving. I would never . . ."

She takes another drag on the cigarette. I can see her squinting against the smoke, her dark brows drawing together in concentration. Uncrossing my legs, I sit up, feet flat on the floor, elbows on knees.

"But your father and I have decided that . . . living together right now is counterproductive."

My grip is loosening. The phone barely touches my ear.

"We're too—too angry with each other, and too uncertain about what to do. So your father . . . he agreed to leave. He's staying at a motel near his office right now."

I tell myself I saw it coming. I thought they were happy, but they weren't. Or maybe happiness isn't enough. I think of the parents of my friends, who yell at each other and then say I love you.

"Ginnie? I'm sorry. If you want to come home now, it's all right. But if you want to stay there, I understand. Ginnie?"

I hang up, push my feet into the sandals, and walk to the front door. Grandma comes out of the kitchen as I shove open the screen door.

"Ginnie," she calls. "Where are you going? Ginnie, don't you want to talk?"

The door slams shut, and I stride down the walk to the street. The hot, humid air clamps around me, and sweat coats my back before I've gone even a few yards up the hill.

They had this all planned, I think. Grandma knew. She probably knew before I got there. Maybe even Tom knew. But I didn't know. Nobody told me. I just got shuttled around from camp last year to Grandma's this year, and nobody told me anything.

My sandals smack the pavement, each step jarring my body. What do I care what they do? What do I care that they were all in on this little conspiracy? If they don't want me, then I don't want them.

I reach the top of the hill and turn right. It's after

seven and most of the stores are closed. At the end of the block, though, a few teenagers lounge in front of one open door. Lenny's.

I stuff my hands in my pockets, searching for money. About forty cents in change and four one-dollar bills. Maybe I can bum some more change off someone or get a couple of dollars changed at Lenny's and buy a pack of cigarettes. The Kents I bought last week are only half gone, but they're in my bedroom and I want a cigarette now.

My hands still in my pockets, I stroll toward Lenny's. A dark-green car, several years old and rusty, sits by the curb, its radio turned up loud. I can make out a song by Bon Jovi. One boy, leaning against the aluminum storefront, sees me and stares challengingly. I try to picture what he is seeing. A lanky girl in jeans that ride on protruding hip bones, and a cropped top that covers small breasts and reveals a stretch of skin at the waist. I keep on walking, meeting his stare. He is smoking a cigarette, and I decide what to do.

Stopping a couple of feet away from him, I call, "Hey, got a cigarette?"

He doesn't move. The other kids are watching us. I don't look away from him. He reminds me of Denny, cool and intriguing, but humor glints in Denny's eyes. This boy looks nasty.

"Yeah, I got a cigarette," he says, sticking his lit one between his lips. "What's it to ya?"

I shrug. "I'll take one, if you can spare it."

"Yeah? What'll you give me for it?"

I hesitate. It occurs to me that this guy is older than I

thought. It occurs to me that I shouldn't have started this conversation. It occurs to me that I should turn around and walk away. "Nothing."

He laughs, a hoarse, jerky sound. "Nothin'. She's going to give me nothin'." He grins at his friends, then turns back to me. His gaze slides up and down my body. "That looks about what you're worth. But hey, I'm a nice guy."

Straightening away from the building, he reaches into the pocket of his denim jacket. "I'll give you a cigarette"—he pulls a pack out—"if you give me a kiss."

"All right."

He walks over and hands me a cigarette. He's shorter than me, and smells of old sweat. "Here you go. Now . . ."

I swiftly kiss his cheek and step back. "There."

Behind him, his friends laugh. "Gotcha there, Jeff," one of them says.

Jeff sneers. "You think you're cute," he says to me. He comes toward me. I step back. "Real cute. Give me that cigarette."

I shake my head. "We made a deal."

"That wasn't the kind of kiss I meant."

"You didn't specify."

"'You didn't specify,'" he mimics in an awful, squeaky voice. "Christ, are you some kind of mutant?"

I'm tempted to ask if he knows what mutant means, but I've scared myself enough with my recklessness. "Listen, it's just a cigarette. Not that big a deal."

"That's 'cause you didn't pay for it." He maneuvers me back against the building, trapping me with his body and arms. Trying not to seem frightened, I keep looking down at him, since I am taller. "But you're going to pay for it now."

He quickly presses his body against mine and kisses me. His mouth open, lips wet and bruising, he thrusts his tongue far back, and my stomach heaves as I try not to gag. That's enough for him. He lets me go and steps back. I wipe his saliva from my mouth and stare at him. He shifts his weight onto one leg, staring back.

"There," he says, "we're even."

I know I could make it worse. I could say enduring a kiss like that is worth five or six cigarettes. But a bit of sanity remains, and I merely nod and stick the cigarette between my lips. I have matches in my pocket and am thankful there's no breeze as I light the cigarette. Jeff watches all of this, and nods as I blow out a plume of smoke.

"What's your name?" he asks.

"Charlotte."

"Yeah? You're kind of cute, Charlotte. I don't remember seein' you before. You go to the high school?"

"No. I go to a private school in New England. My parents don't like having me around much."

He nods. "Yeah. My folks can't wait to get rid of me either. Listen, I got some beer and my friends and me are gonna have a little party. You wanna come along?"

Don't do it, I tell myself, glancing at his friends. There are two boys and three girls. Another car sits behind the rusty green one now. Its radio is playing loud too, and Billy Joel is insisting in stereo that we didn't start the fire.

I'm not completely stupid. I know I shouldn't get into

the car of some boy I don't know. Denny never forced me in any way, but he didn't need to. He knew I'd keep giving in little by little. This guy . . .

I can still taste his kiss. Denny I could handle, but Jeff is bigger, older, with that nastiness in his eyes. I remind myself of a story that went around my school this spring, about a girl who got stoned at a party and passed out and didn't even notice that three or four guys had sex with her. But this is like a game of chicken, I think. Who will blink first? Me? Jeff? My parents?

"Sure, I'll come along," I say.

He smiles. "All right. Hey, guys. This is Charlotte. She's coming along with us."

The guys nod, smiling. The girls give me the once-over. "Fine," one of the guys says. "You got the beer, Jeff?"

"Yeah, I got the beer."

"Then let's go."

We all start for the two cars. Two of the girls and one boy scramble into the back of the green car. Jeff walks around to the driver's side.

"Get in, Charlotte."

I grasp the open door. The metal is hot. Jeff starts the engine, coaxing it until it revs loudly, then settles into an unsteady rumbling. The sound reminds me of Denny's motorcycle. He'll be angry if I go out with another guy. Then I remember the letter, remember my mother saying it's all right if I want to come home. I slip one leg into the car, then stop, glance back. I thought I saw someone coming to get me. But when I turn, no one is there.

I get in the car and slam the door shut.

E L E V E N

This night is far, far worse than the night of the reckless driving. Then at least I had some control. Now I have none and neither does Jeff. We left Lenny's at about seven-thirty, and by nine he's drunk six beers, on top of several shots of Jack Daniels. He seems to be driving okay, but I wish he'd keep both hands on the wheel, and not one on my thigh.

I have no idea where we are, though some sense of direction tells me we're not far from Grandma's. From Lenny's we cruised around neighborhoods I'd never been in before, finally reaching a park. As we sped along the narrow streets, the other car that was with us, the one with just a guy and girl in it, disappeared. Jeff laughed when he saw that, and the guy in the backseat of our car grunted a few times, like he was having sex. The girls laughed; then one of them squealed when the guy threw himself on her, pressing her against the back of the seat, and kissed her. That was when Jeff's hand became glued to my thigh.

By the time Jeff throws his seventh beer can out the window, I'm trying hard to think of some way out of this. I'm about to ask to stop at a gas station so I can go to the bathroom, when Jeff squeezes my thigh and says, "Let's dump these jerks and crawl into the backseat together. Just you and me. Huh, Charlotte?"

"Do it in the front seat," the guy in back suggests. "We won't mind."

"You're sick, Sam," one of the girls says, but the other girl, the one he kissed, laughs and says, "We'll just have our own party in the backseat."

"All right!" Sam yells, and out of the corner of my eye I see him grab her breast. She giggles again and pulls him back on top of her to kiss him. The other girl turns to look out her window, either embarrassed or bored.

"Look, Jeff," I say. "I think—"

"Hey, come on, Charlotte." He glances at me, and his hand slides on the wheel, jerking the car. "We're just gonna have a little fun. Move over here." He tugs on my thigh. "Move over here and give me a kiss."

"Uh, Jeff . . . Maybe you should concentrate on your driving."

He laughs. Not a hoarse, joking laugh, but a hard, ominous one. "You know, you're a real tease."

His hand slides up my thigh to my crotch. I squirm away, pressing hard against the door. My heart pounds against my ribs and I can't control my breathing. I'm scared.

He laughs again, even more nastily. "Bet you're a virgin. Whaddya think, Sam? Think she's a virgin?"

Sam's got the girl on his lap, her top off. Even as his hand scoops her breast out of her bra, he gives me an assessing look. "I don't know, but I'd be glad to find out for you."

"Hey!" the girl exclaims. "What about me?"

"You?" He pinches her breast. "I know you're not a virgin."

As shocked as I am by what's going on in the backseat, I'm also grateful it's captured Jeff's attention. He adjusts the rearview mirror so he can see them.

"Yeah," he says. "We know she ain't no virgin."

I face front, not looking, trying not to listen as the girl sighs and moans. They won't do much, I think, not in a moving car with three other people around. Then I hear a zipper rasp, and blood pours into my face. They won't—

"Yeah," Jeff says hoarsely, still watching in the mirror. "Show it to me, baby."

I hear Sam grunt, the girl squeal, then Jeff grabs my thigh again, hauling me over to him. A dizzying haze explodes in my brain, like a sudden cloudburst. I feel faint. Sam's telling the girl to touch him, to do it hard, and she's telling him—

"Shit!" Jeff yells, and slams on the brakes.

I'm thrown against the dashboard. Behind me I hear cries and curses, and the front seat bounces from the force of three bodies crashing into it. There's a moment of eerie silence, as if we're all checking that we're alive. Cautiously I look up.

The car is off the road, its front bumper no more than

an inch from a telephone pole. Sitting up, I glance at Jeff. His face is white and he's staring wide-eyed, not at the pole but in the rearview mirror. I glance behind me, wondering if I'll see broken bodies, faces contorted with pain.

No. The other three look as awful as Jeff, but they're okay. Then I look beyond them. At the police car. At its flashing lights. At the two men getting out of it, walking toward us.

"Get dressed," Jeff hisses.

The girl and Sam fumble with their clothes as one officer appears at Jeff's window. Swiveling around, I see the other one beside me. He shines his flashlight into the car, catching the girl still half undressed, then glancing the light off my face. I know he must see my fear, but he'll think I'm afraid of him, not of Jeff. Instinctively I shove the door open, nearly hitting him, and scramble out.

"Stay in the car," he orders.

"No way." I lean against the car, breathing quickly, my legs barely steady enough to keep me upright.

The officer—his tag says Lawrence—apparently figures I'm not a threat, and shines his light again on the backseat. "You three okay?" he asks.

They must have nodded. He straightens and looks across the hood to the other officer, who's asking Jeff for his license and car registration.

"Look, officer," Jeff says, "I can explain. See, Charlotte, that girl who was in the front seat, said she wasn't feeling well—"

"Your license, please."

I glance over, avoiding Officer Lawrence's gaze. I can't see Jeff, but I see the officer take something from him and study it in the beam of his flashlight. "Step out of the car, please."

He stands back as Jeff pushes the door open. He gets out okay, but can't stand up straight without putting one hand on the hood.

"Have you been drinking tonight?" the officer asks.

"Well, yeah. A couple of beers."

"A couple?"

"Sure. Not enough to make me drunk, you know. I was just taking my friends home when Sh-shar . . . uh, *Char*lotte said she was feelin' sick. She sounded really awful, you know, so I glanced over at her to see if she was okay. I must have jerked the wheel, and that's how I ran off the road." He shrugged. "Nothing serious."

"Mr. Wade, do you know what the speed limit is on this road?"

"Huh?" Jeff looks around, as if not certain what road he's on. "Uh, yeah. It's forty-five, right?"

"No, Mr. Wade. It's thirty. We've been following you for approximately two miles, and you were averaging fifty miles an hour. You were also weaving across the road even before you ran off it. I suspect you've had more than 'a couple of beers,' Mr. Wade, and I'd like you to take a sobriety test."

"Hey, sure. No problem."

He fails it, of course. The officers aren't inclined to let any of us drive. They radio for another cop car and a wrecker. When the other cops arrive, Jeff and I are ushered into the backseat of the first car, while the other three are squeezed into the back of the second. Jeff

96

doesn't speak to me as we drive off.

The police station is in the town's municipal building, about five blocks from Grandma's house. The policemen tell us to sit on the benches in the grim tile hallway, then they start calling parents. Jeff is taken away for his breathalizer test, so they'll know if he was over the legal alcohol limit.

The rest of us just sit there, waiting. The girl who was making out with Sam is crying. Sam growls at her to shut up, and an officer growls the same thing at him.

Numbed, exhausted, and scared, I sit hunched over, elbows on knees and hands holding my head. I know why I did it, why I got in Jeff's car, but that why does not easily turn into blame on my parents' heads. My dad's moving out isn't a good excuse for nearly getting myself raped. I wanted independence. I wanted freedom. I got it.

Grandma arrives first, before the other kids' parents. She walks slowly down the hall, head high but chin trembling. Beside her is Mr. Weber. Of course. Who else would she call to come with her?

I stand when I see her, but Officer Lawrence tells me to sit back down. He walks across the hall to Grandma and gently takes her arm, leading her back up the hall, away from us sitting on the bench. He bends down to talk to her, and she doesn't move, not even to nod her head. At last she murmurs something to him, and he escorts her back to me.

"You can go now, Miss Ryan," he says. "But I would like to warn you that what happened tonight could have had much more serious repercussions. I'm not just talking about almost hitting that telephone pole. I'm talking about what was happening inside the car."

I frown, wondering how he knew, and his lips thin into a grim smile. "We were behind you for a while," he explains. "We could see what was going on in the backseat. And your girlfriend there didn't have her shirt on."

Shame and fear wash over me, knocking down what is left of my feeble defenses and self-esteem. I want to run into his arms and have him hold me as my father would, confess that I was stupid and deserve whatever happened, and have him tell me that no one will ever hurt me. Maybe he sees some of that in my face, because he walks over to me and takes my arm, urging me up from the bench. Trying to keep my shoulders straight and head up, I allow him to lead me to Grandma.

Reaching her, I chance one glance at her face. There is no forgiveness there. I see pain and sadness and anger. Tears prick my eyes, and I blink and look away.

"I'm sorry, Grandma," I mumble.

She draws herself up, taller than me for the first time in years. "We'll talk about this in the morning, Virginia."

With Mr. Weber following us, we leave the police station.

I sleep fitfully all night, dozing off as I worry about how to explain to Grandma, to my parents, even to Kris; then jerking awake as scary dreams of sex and Jeff and his friends weave around me. As I lie in the dark, I realize it's not the sex that shocked me. Of course I know people have sex. It was their shamelessness, the strangeness of their doing it, starting to do it, in a car with other people

98

around. To want something so badly, to be so driven by it, is frightening.

In the morning I face Grandma. She is at the dining-room table with her coffee, and I stand behind my chair, head down. She looks bad, not at all cheery as she usually is in the morning. Her eyes aren't bright, her hair isn't well combed, and she buttoned the blouse beneath her jumper crooked. She looks tired and disappointed.

"Grandma," I whisper, "I don't know what to say."

She makes that little movement of hers, straightening her body from the waist up. She does that whenever she's uncomfortable with a conversation. "The officer who spoke to me last night"—she doesn't look at me, but at the picture of some female ancestor hanging above the side table—"told me he didn't think you were in that car willingly."

"Uh . . . not exactly. I—he—the guy who was driving the car saw me walking and asked if I wanted to go for a drive. I . . . uh . . ." I bend my head lower so I can watch my finger trace the design carved into the back of the dining-room chair. "I was mad and upset, and I wasn't thinking very clearly, so I went."

"Why didn't you just come home?"

"Because—because I was upset. I wanted . . . to do something wrong."

She nods. Yes, it must sound familiar. All parents must have to deal with this.

"And then?" she asks.

"I couldn't get away. I wanted to. I asked him to stop at a gas station so I could use the bathroom, and I figured

I'd just run off and find a bus or something to get me back here, but he wouldn't stop. I didn't even know where we were by the time the . . . uh, the cops found us. Getting in his car was a mistake and I regret it a lot, but I didn't do anything wrong other than that."

She sighs and drains her coffee cup. When she sets it down, the china clicking softly, she looks even more weary. "You're not my daughter," she says, startling me. It sounds as if she's disowning me. "It's up to your parents to decide what your punishment should be."

So we call Mom, but she's not home. Grandma doesn't want to call Dad at his office. "I'll keep trying your mother," she says, and carries the phone out to her chair in the living room. I disappear into the garden, unable to face her sad blue eyes any longer.

I sit in a corner of the garden, under the shade of a lilac tree, motionless and silent, trying to purge all memories of last night. I must have dozed off, because I jerk when I hear Grandma calling me.

"Your mother's on the phone," she's saying.

I trudge up the stone steps to the house. I take the phone from her and drop down onto the couch, same as last night. "Hi, Mom."

"Ginnie." She pauses. "Why did you do it?"

This is the worst part. Confessing not to the crime, but to whatever nastiness inside me that made me do it. Flaunting Denny is average on the scale of teenage rebellion. Getting into a car with a stranger rates much higher.

"Because I'm stupid," I say. That's a good excuse. "And . . ." And what? I'm born to be wild, born to be bad? That's not fair. It wasn't all my fault. "And because I was angry and wanted to hurt . . . I don't know, hurt you or hurt me."

Angry, I repeat silently. I told her I was angry.

"Were you hurt?" she asks.

I'm surprised and decide to try some more honesty. "I was . . . I was scared." God, now I sound like a little kid, running home to Mommy because the big kids teased her. Maybe I should aim for some coolness with the honesty. "I thought it was going to get a lot worse, and it probably would have if the cops hadn't stopped us."

"Worse how?"

I lift one foot up onto the couch so I can push back the thick cuticle on my big toe. "The guy who was driving, he . . . uh, wanted something more than just a kiss."

"I see."

Her quiet, almost hesitant voice puzzles me as much as my honesty. She's not yelling, she's not ordering me to my room and telling me to stay there for the next week. Why not?

"Is this the sort of independence you want?" she asks.

"Mom . . ." I feel that jab in my heart. Tears fill and overflow my eyes. I swipe at them, but they keep falling, leaking from the corners of my eyes. I swallow a sob, breathing hard to hold it in.

"No." I hold the phone away and sniffle loudly, then speak to her again. "I was just stupid. I told you that. I was angry and not thinking. It was just something to do because I didn't want to . . . Why did you do it?" I suddenly shout. "Why did you make him leave? And why did you make me leave too? Do you hate both of us?"

"Ginnie, no." Her voice is quiet, deep. She might be

calming me from a nightmare. "I don't hate you. I never have, I never could. Maybe I should have been more honest with you about how things stood between your father and me, but I believed that—that we might be able to work things out. I didn't want to worry you unnecessarily."

"I wouldn't have worried," I mutter. "Maybe I could have helped."

"No. It's between your father and me. We love both you and Tom very much, and the last thing we want to do is lose either of you. But right now, it's best for us to be apart for a little while."

We're both silent. I rub my cheek against my shoulder, drying the tears. The anger has faded as quickly as it grew, and it's easier to breathe now. Easier than it's been since last night.

"Well," she says at last, "what you did was wrong. You know that. You worried your grandmother, and you could have been badly hurt. You know that, too. Grandma told me she's been letting you drive Grandpa's car alone. We'll stop that for now. You can drive her if she needs to go someplace, but don't take the car by yourself until she tells you it's all right. And whenever you go off somewhere, even if it's just across the street to mail a letter, tell her where you're going and when you'll be back."

"All right." I take a deep breath of relief. This is not harsh punishment at all. "Thanks."

She laughs. "You're welcome. Ginnie, I'm sorry. Sorry this summer has been such a mess for you. And I'm very glad you weren't hurt last night. I know sometimes you think I don't care what happens to you, but that's not true. I do care."

"Yeah." My voice wobbles. I'm going to cry again.

"I'll give your father a call later and tell him. I'm sure he'll want to talk to you. And Ginnie, you can call anytime you want to talk. And you can still come home whenever you'd like."

She asks to talk to Grandma again. I drop the phone onto the couch, walk through the kitchen to get Grandma, then return to the garden, not the least bit interested in eavesdropping.

After I wash the dinner dishes that night, I take the radio out into the backyard. Grandma and I are not talking, but not because of anger. Sadness and the need to adjust to a possible new family structure keeps us wandering the house with downcast eyes, not speaking for fear our bewilderment and helplessness will engulf us.

Tonight she sits in the living room, sipping tea and leafing through a photo album. Her vision has gotten so bad in the past couple of years that the images must be too blurry for her to distinguish. But perhaps she knows each picture so well, she sees it better in her memory than she ever did in reality.

Sitting in the yard, I play with the radio dial and find a ball game. Baseball games all sound the same, and the announcers' voices, their comments, the muffled groans and cheers of the crowd, are no different tonight from all the other summer nights when I would sit here with Grandpa, listening to this same radio. Sometimes the Pirates won, but Grandpa never let on that it pleased him. He'd just say in his slow voice, "Well, I guess I'll go to bed now."

Tonight the Pirates are up four to three in the top of the seventh. The first two Philadelphia Phillies batters strike out; the third works his way to a count of two and two. Here comes the pitch, the swing . . . and it's a line drive toward center field, picked off by the shortstop. He throws to first for an easy out, and the Pirates still lead four to three.

Makes for a simple life.

I find a rock station, listening as Bruce Springsteen rasps his way through "Born to Run." I nod in agreement, thinking I might as well run to the nearest exit myself. After all, I'm not doing so well here. My parents are creating new lives for themselves. My turn next. They could have waited one more year, though, before this separation, this first step to divorce. Then I'd be in college, gone and not needing a home anymore.

No home. I try out the feel of that, picturing myself in ten years, grown up, worldly, wearing a business suit and meeting my father for lunch. We talk about our respective jobs, our respective apartments, a bit of family gossip.

Or I'll live overseas, have a flat in London, go to plays and parties, and only come home for Christmas.

That's not so bad. There's a freedom when you let go of convention. "My parents are divorced," I'll tell people, "so I don't really have a family to go home to. And I'm not interested in marriage. I'm happy enough alone."

The hell with you all, I think.

The DJ's voice explodes out of the radio. The Pirates lost, giving up two runs in the ninth inning. Final score, five to four.

"Well," I say into the darkness, "I guess I'll go to bed now."

T W E L V E

Diane calls the next morning. I wonder if she's heard about me and Jeff and the police, and is calling so we can compare notes on the police station.

"What a drag," she'll say. "Nothing to do there while you sit and wait for your parents. Just all those cops standing around, looking superior."

"Yeah," I'll say, "and they really could use a new interior decorator. That color scheme is lousy. And they could put cushions on the benches. They're awfully hard."

But I guess she didn't hear, because she says nothing about it. She just wants to know if I can come over and visit. She's been grounded only a few days, but she's totally bored. I say all right.

She doesn't live far away, and I can walk there. When I

tell Grandma where I'm going, she draws herself up straight and studies me for a moment. Obviously she's suspicious of this girl Diane. I've got to give her credit for good instincts.

"All right." She peers at her elegant silver wristwatch. "It's ten o'clock now. Be home by noon."

I almost grimace at the order, then nod and say okay.

Diane's house is smaller than Grandma's, crowded together with identical houses on a long block. It looks like where I live. Her mother, a woman with severely short hair and a cotton shirt and skirt, answers the door. She smiles and says, "Yes? Can I help you?"

"Hi," I say. "Is Diane here?"

Her mouth flattens instantly. Harsh lines cut deep down her cheeks. "Yes, she's here. And you are . . . ?"

"My name is Ginnie Ryan. I live with my grand-mother over on Spruce Road."

She steps back, holding the screen door open. "Come in."

It's dark inside, curtains drawn against the summer sun. The couch and two easy chairs are upholstered in dull shades of brown, and the carpeting is about as plush as Astroturf.

"Diane's in her room," Mrs. LaSalle says, leading me to the stairs on the far side of the living room.

We walk up, and I hear music pounding through the walls. Michael Jackson. Mrs. LaSalle shakes her head. At the top of the stairs she turns left and knocks hard on a closed door.

"Diane!"

"What!"

Diane yanks the door open; synthesized music assaults

106

us. She glares at her mother, then sees me. "Hey. You came. Come on in."

Mrs. LaSalle wants to say something, but doesn't seem to know what. Her indecisiveness as she looks at both of us, swinging her body first toward me, then back at her daughter, would be funny if not for her angry expression. She looks as though she's been angry for years. Finally, her mouth tight again, she steps around me and goes back downstairs. Diane rolls her eyes and pulls me into her room.

She turns the music down and asks, "Isn't my mother weird?"

I shrug, glancing around. "What mother isn't?"

The room is small and messy and oddly unsettling. Vivid posters of Guns N' Roses and M. C. Hammer clash with little-girl furniture. Across the top of her French provincial dresser, silver bracelets and dozens of funky earrings surround dusty perfume bottles, an open jewelry box, and six bottles of nail polish, all nearly empty. Clothes trail from the gold-handled drawers. A ruffled white spread lies crumpled at the foot of her unmade bed.

Even Diane is unsettling. Wearing cotton shorts and a pink tank top, she's not the tough, confident shoplifter. Her hair's tamed into a ponytail, and I can see freckles that she must usually hide with makeup. She's the girl who helped me when I was sick at the pool, not the one arrested for reckless driving. I wonder how many other personalities she has.

"So how ya doin'?" she asks, bouncing onto her bed and sitting cross-legged. "Sit down."

She pats the bed, but I choose the desk chair. "I'm okay. How 'bout you?"

"God. You've got to be kidding. I'm about to go crazy. You know, something like this happens and you really find out who your friends are. I mean, hardly anyone's come to see me. It's like I've got the bubonic plague or something. But you know who comes every day?" I shake my head. "Cheryl. Can you believe it? She sits up here and eats M&M's and tells me what everyone did the night before. Shit. She just makes me feel worse."

"I'm sorry. How much longer are you going to be grounded?"

"I've lost track. Who cares anyhow? Even when I'm un-grounded, I'm not allowed to see Larry. I might as well just stay in here."

"Yeah, that's rough."

She looks at me. "That guy I've seen you with, at the pool and that night, is he your boyfriend?"

I shake my head. "No. He's just this guy who lives across the street from my grandmother. I had a boyfriend back in Philadelphia, but he just broke up with me."

"What a jerk. How come?"

"He was feeling lonely, I guess, so he started going out with this other girl." I hesitate, then say with some non-chalance, "She's probably sleeping with him."

Diane picks at a torn fingernail. They're bright pink today. "Guys sure think that's important."

"They sure do."

We're silent as the last song ends. The tape player clicks off, and we both stare at it.

"Well . . ." I say.

"Don't go."

Diane speaks quickly, anxiously, as if she fears being

108

left alone. "Tell me honestly." She leans forward. "What do you think of Larry?"

I shrug. "I wasn't really around him that long, you know. I mean, he's cute." She nods. "He seems okay."

"Yeah." She smiles. The corners of her eyes crinkle, and I realize I've never seen her smile before. "We've been going out for five months now. He loves me, you know. He really does. He told me on our second date that he was falling in love with me. And I knew I was falling in love with him."

She smiles again, a sappy smile all people in love seem to get. "I remember the night he told me he loved me. It was the night of the junior prom, May thirteenth." She falls back on the unmade bed. "He wore a white tux and he looked gorgeous. We were driving home and he told me he loved me. He told me I was beautiful."

I know what's coming and almost tell her to stop. I don't want to hear this.

"We drove to this place we always go to and we start, you know, kissing and stuff. Then he tells me he bought some rubbers, and if we love each other we should make love. It's only natural."

She props herself up on her elbows. "And he was right. Oh God, it was so great. I hadn't been sure before then that I loved him, but I knew then. You just . . . you just know."

Perhaps I look like I don't believe her, for she abruptly sits up and leans closer to me. "You're still a virgin, aren't you? You wouldn't understand."

"No," I say. "I mean, yes, I am a virgin, and no, I don't understand." Sam and that girl flash through my mind. Sex, not love. I really don't understand.

"Then you're right," Diane says. "That's probably why your boyfriend broke up with you."

Her tone is so superior, I want to hit her. "I *know* that's why he broke up with me. But I didn't love him, so I wasn't going to have sex with him."

The conversation has slipped too far into falseness. Diane is pretending to be an adult who knows all about love and sex, and I am caught in the game with her, using those words as if they make sense to me. The simple truth is I didn't sleep with Denny because I was scared. Scared like a child, when I was afraid to close my eyes after a nightmare, certain something dreadful was waiting to catch me as soon as I let my guard down and trusted the darkness. And once it caught me, I would carry the nightmare with me and never be only myself again.

We stare angrily at each other for a moment, then she turns away. "Yeah, well," she mutters, "maybe you're right."

"Right about what?"

"Not sleeping with a guy." Her shoulders slump and her tough defiance is gone again. "You know, I thought once Larry heard I was grounded, he'd start figuring out ways to see me. Go behind my mother's back, you know? But he didn't. I haven't talked to him once. Cheryl told me he's been grounded for a week and his parents won't let him use his car anymore. Not for six months." She looks up at me, her eyes large with tears. "I don't care if he can't drive anywhere. I don't even care if we can't be alone together. I just want to see him and talk to him. I want him to tell me he still loves me."

She jumps off the bed and storms across the room to her dresser. On it is a framed photograph of her and Larry. He's in a white tux; she's in a short black lace dress. She picks it up and stares at it, rubbing the back of her hand over her eyes. "Cheryl said—"

She flings the picture at the closed door. The metal frame gouges the paint and the glass shatters, sprinkling onto the floor. I stare, stunned by her violence. Before I can move or speak, her mother shouts Diane's name.

"What are you doing in there?" she yells.

Diane yanks the door open. "Nothing!" she shouts down the hall. "I just dropped something!"

Her mother doesn't answer, and Diane slams the door shut. "Christ," she mutters, looking down at the remains of the picture. "Hey listen. I'm sorry about what I said about your boyfriend. He's a jerk for breaking up with you."

"It's okay. I'm sorry about Larry. I'm sure he still loves you, but . . . well, it's tough for both of you."

"Yeah, yeah." She slouches down onto the bed again. "You don't have to leave right now, do you? Can you stay a little while longer?"

"Well . . ."

She jumps off the bed again and reaches around me, pulling open a desk drawer. "Do you know how to play poker?" she asks, holding up a deck of cards. "Or we could play Monopoly."

"Not Monopoly. I always lose. But I do know how to play poker." I stand and walk over to her tape collection. "Let's put some more music on."

T H I R T E E N

"Hello, Ginger."

It's Dad. Only he calls me that.

"How are you?" he asks.

"Fine. Creamed somebody at five-card stud today."

He laughs. "Not literally, I hope."

"What? Oh, no. Not literally."

He pauses. "I guess you had a little trouble the other night."

I pause, too, then whisper, "Yeah." I was able to ignore my pain over this family separation while I was talking to Mom, but now I wish Dad were here. He rarely shows emotion, and never talks with me about how I'm feeling, but when he knows I'm upset, knows I need company more than I need to talk, he always finds the right thing to do. Like taking me ice skating on a Saturday night when my friends are at a party I'm not invited to. Or taking me out for dessert the night I brought home a report card with a "D" in physics.

I frown, remembering all this. After everything we've shared, how did this happen?

"Dad . . . I was just thinking . . . Well, I'm sorry for what I did two nights ago, and sorry—sorry that I haven't been very . . . good, not a good daughter this past year."

He lets out a long breath. "Ginnie, you're a wonderful daughter. Don't ever think that anything you've said or done is the cause of your mother and me . . . separating. That's something she and I take full blame for."

"But—" But what? But you did it all wrong? I was *supposed* to have some effect on you? You were supposed to be a solid, stable unit that I could break away from when I was ready? And then come back whenever I wanted? You weren't supposed to leave first.

"Ginnie, this isn't easy for any of us. Your mother and I tried, but it wasn't right. In the end . . . well, nothing's final yet, but this is the best for all of us."

His vagueness doesn't surprise me. That's the thing about Dad. He'll take you so far and then stop, and you have to stitch together the bits he told you, hoping you get the whole picture of what he meant.

"Are you thinking of when you'll come back?" he asks.

"I kind of like it here, Dad."

"All your friends are here. What about Denny?"

I say nothing for a moment. My stomach clenches, though thank God I don't cry. That pain has dulled

113

against the edge of the other night's insanity.

"We broke up, Dad. Or he broke up with me. It doesn't matter."

"I'm sorry, honey." He pauses. "I liked Denny."

"What? You liked him? I thought everybody hated him."

"No . . . Well, your mother did worry about you when you were with him." He chuckles, a sound so normal, so Dadlike, I believe for a moment nothing has changed. "But he always reminded me of myself when I was his age."

"Really? You had a motorcycle?"

"Absolutely. I thought I was pretty cool riding around on that."

"Did you have a black leather jacket?"

"Yep. I was a regular JD."

"Why, Dad, a man after my own heart. But it's okay about Denny. It's not like I expected to marry him, you know."

"Good. You're too young even to think about marriage. Don't get married until you're at least thirty."

"I won't tell Grandma you said that. She thinks all the good men will be gone by the time I'm twenty-two."

"You will never lack for men, Ginnie."

I almost answer sarcastically, then realize he's serious. Uncertain how to handle a compliment I can't believe, I say in my best Southern accent, "One Sunday afternoon I received *seventeen* gentlemen callers!" I played Amanda Wingfield in *The Glass Menagerie* in drama class last year.

Dad laughs. He knows the play. "Oh, at least," he says.

After I hang up I turn to see Grandma standing in the archway between the living room and dining room. "That was Dad. He says hi."

She crosses the room to her chair and sits. "How was your visit with your friend today?"

"It was good. She's a little lonely these days. She's . . . uh, been grounded for a couple of weeks."

Grandma doesn't seem surprised. "What did she do?"

"She and her boyfriend were caught speeding, so her mother grounded her and won't let her see her boyfriend again."

Grandma stares straight at me, as if considering if my own punishment is severe enough. I fidget and look down, remembering the gray walls of the police station, the echoing male voices, the girl crying beside me. How long until the memory doesn't make me shudder?

"Maybe not seeing her boyfriend is for the best," Grandma says finally.

"I agree." And I do. Larry reminds me too much of Denny. "She says she's in love with him," I go on, "but I think seventeen is too young to be in love. Don't you?"

Grandma lifts her gaze to over my head. "I suppose for some girls it is. Other girls are ready to be in love. There's nothing wrong with waiting, though. Your heart will let you know. You just have to listen to it."

I've read that line in books. The man says to the reluctant woman, "But what does your heart tell you?" Of course her heart tells her she's in love with him, and of course it all works out, but what about when your heart and reality can't get it together?

"Why didn't you marry Charles?" I ask abruptly.

She crosses her legs, smoothing her stocking up one of them. "Charles?"

"Yes, Charles. You know, the guy with the beautiful blue eyes and the nicest smile."

"Don't be smart, Ginnie," she scolds, turning to look at the tall vase I filled with snapdragons that morning.

"Come on, Grandma," I coax, eager to talk about anything that has nothing to do with speeding cars or ex-boyfriends or separated parents. "Tell me. What happened between you two?"

"Nothing."

"Nothing? You said you were in love with him."

"Oh . . ." She laughs. At that moment I understand that Grandma lies with that little laugh of hers. She hopes to distract you, to convince you that whatever you're talking about is unimportant, or harmless, or painless. "I was so young and it was all a little foolish. We were not . . . well suited to each other."

"I can't imagine that ever stopped anyone from falling in love."

She glances at me. "You've been reading too many of those horrid paperback novels of yours. There are certain people—men—who just are not *right*. Oh, you may be intrigued by them, but you won't really love them. Not the way you love the man who will be your husband."

"You mean the first time I fall in love, I'm supposed to marry the guy?"

"No." Her look warns me I'm being smart again. "When you meet the man you'll marry, you'll understand that what you felt for any other man was only infatuation."

"But at the time I'll think I love them, and will tell them that. Then when I *really* fall in love, I'll have to go back to them and say, 'Oops. It was a mistake. I didn't love you.'"

"Don't be silly. Of course you don't go back and tell them."

"But I would have lied to them."

She doesn't answer, and I ponder this. Love implies to me a desire to marry. I cannot see telling every person I date that I love him. That would destroy the word and the emotion. But how do you know when you should say it? Do the words simply spring from you, an uncontrollable urge? Or should you not say them at all, not take the risk?

The songs I listen to warn me that love slips by so swiftly, trustless and deceiving. Life's too damaging, and love too often the first casualty. We all sleep alone, one singer says, while another asks why would she want a heart, when hearts can be broken.

I believe the songs, have learned to expect unhappiness in love, and for a moment I am sure an unfettered, loves-lost life is my fate—and for the best. I look at Grandma. She is motionless, her expression melancholy.

"Why didn't you marry Charles?" I ask again, softly.

She doesn't move or speak for a moment. I'm sure she will still refuse to tell me, but then she says, "I couldn't." I feel the ache of love, decades old but still there. "He already had a wife. Oh, she was quite ill. Tuberculosis. I heard later that she died, but . . . it was too late." She pauses, forcing brightness back into her eyes and voice. "I'm sure nothing would have come of it even if he hadn't been married. He was a little . . . wild. Not at all steady

117

and secure like your grandfather." She turns to me. "And I loved your grandfather. Much more than I loved Charles. I loved Charles in a different way, a young way. It was . . . just a bit of madness."

I can see them, the handsome blue-eyed man and my tiny blond grandmother, racing toward each other along a windy, cold Pittsburgh street, racing into each other's arms. They would laugh, and for as long as they were together the real world wouldn't exist.

Had they been lovers? No, I cannot see Grandma breaking the rules that far. Yet perhaps she had. Knowing the love was hopeless, perhaps they had taken what they could, then let it go. And she had gone on.

I know she loved my grandfather, and he loved her. They argued constantly, yet I always felt a link between them, unbreakable and immutable. When he died, we feared she would die as well, of loneliness and a broken heart.

"I'm sorry," I say.

She smiles. "It wouldn't have worked anyhow," she repeats. "A love like that . . . it's too strong. It burns itself out too quickly."

She pushes herself up. "I'd like a ginger ale float. How about you?"

Kris calls just before I go to bed that night. He sounds awkward as he asks how I am, then adds that his dad told him about what happened the other night.

"You're okay?" he asks.

"Yeah. Nothing happened. Nothing much."

Nothing much. Images sweep through my mind, the

memory of the voices, the words, the sounds.

"I'm okay," I say, just to make sure.

He hesitates, then says, "I saw you leave the house that night. I started to come after you, just to talk. . . . But you looked so angry, I figured you didn't want to see me."

I remember looking back before I got in Jeff's car, thinking I'd seen someone. It was Kris. I realize that I'd wanted to see Kris running to save me.

"Well." I exhale heavily. "I'm okay now."

"I'm glad." Another pause, then he asks, "Would you like to come for dinner tomorrow night?"

Startled, I'm silent for a moment. Sitting at another family's dinner table, eating their favorite foods, following their particular rules of etiquette, always flusters me. Denny had me over once, and my discomfort, my out-of-place feeling, had been so intense, I'd hardly been able to eat.

Still, I tell Kris all right.

F O U R T E E N

Nine of us squeeze around the oval table in the Webers' cramped dining room. The room is not small, but as in the living room and kitchen and hallways running between, the furniture and belongings of nine people are stuffed into it. You have to turn sideways to get past anyone.

I sit between Kris and Cara, one seat down from Mr. Weber, a lean, slow, quiet man. Cara, with blond curls, is as sweet and dreamy at fourteen as I was sullen and angry. Nicole sits across from me, her enviably black hair wavy and full. She smiles often, readily and cheerfully, like her mother. So much goodwill makes me feel sullen again.

Mrs. Weber serves bowls of spaghetti and meatballs, long loaves of powerful garlic bread, and a salad of lettuce and tomatoes and Spanish onion and raw mushrooms and green peppers. Two large pitchers of milk anchor the table, one at either end. A tall container of grated Parmesan cheese, two plates of butter, and five salad dressings make their rounds in the wake of the other food. The table is as crowded as the rest of the house, and I'm afraid I will spill my milk, or Kris's, or tip over the basket of garlic bread, or any other disastrous thing.

"How's your grandfather's car?" Eli asks, as I dish out some spaghetti.

"Fine," I say. The eldest of the children, Eli is tall, good-looking, and self-confident. He looks like Kris, except his hair has darkened to a wheat color, and his chest and shoulders have broadened to fit his long arms.

"Your grandfather kept it in perfect condition," he goes on.

I nod and accept the bowl of sauce from Kris. "He didn't drive much, you know."

"This is delicious, Mother," Nicole says.

Mrs. Weber smiles, then quickly turns to the two youngest. "Ian, Aileen, *one* piece of garlic bread. And Aileen, if you don't want any sauce, at least take a meatball."

"No," Aileen says. "I won't eat meat. I'm a vegetable like Nicole."

Everyone laughs, and I glance at Nicole's plate. She dribbled only a little sauce on her spaghetti, no meatballs.

"That's vegetarian, dope," Ian says.

"Mom! He called me—"

"I heard him," Mrs. Weber says mildly, breaking off a piece of garlic bread for herself. "I don't want to hear language like that from you, Ian Alistair Weber. Now apologize to your sister."

"I'm sorry," Ian mumbles into his milk glass.

Aileen sniffles a few times, then forgets the insult as she concentrates on wrapping spaghetti around her fork.

The Webers do not eat in silence. Everyone talks, and Mr. and Mrs. Weber and Eli and Nicole keep looking at me to make sure I'm not lacking either food or conversation. I'm not. Cara wants to know all about where I live and what my school is like and where I think I might go to college, while Kris keeps asking if I want the cheese, the salad dressing, more milk. Mrs. Weber asks about my grandmother and mother, and Mr. Weber tells me to always kick off the high idle on the Dodge before driving it. I barely have time to swallow a bite before someone else is speaking to me.

The Webers are unlike my family, with our flat dinnertime recitations of what we have done that day. Eli talks about cars with his father, while Nicole describes to her mother the folk dress of the Georgian people in the former Soviet Union. Ian and Aileen giggle together, and Kris discusses seriously with Cara the book he is reading—*North to the Orient* by Anne Morrow Lindbergh.

I listen, amazed at the volume and variety of speech, at the easy voices. No back-of-the-throat tension, which afflicts me when I speak to my parents. In my memory all of our family dinners become gray and silent, with the evening news as background noise. I imagine our dining room as chilly, formal, something out of a British farce with four people spaced along a twenty-foot-long table.

Of course it's not true. The room is warm, newly decorated by Mom with golden wallpaper on the upper half of the walls, creamy paint on the bottom, and lots of wood. We sit clustered at one end of the table, Mom and I opposite each other and Dad at the head. Meals are silent now, but they could be lively when Tom and I were kids. When Grandma and Grandpa came for the holidays, Mom sent Tom to the kitchen nearly every night for being silly and giggling at the table. We all knew it was because Grandpa was making faces at him whenever Mom and Grandma weren't looking.

Grandpa's gone, and Grandma doesn't like to travel any longer. Will Mom and Dad and Tom and I ever eat together again?

I glance around the Webers' table. If all families disintegrate as the children grow up and move out, the Webers have plenty of time. Cara, Ian, and Aileen will stay with their parents for years yet, so the older kids will still have a family home to come back to.

I look at Kris. He'll leave in a year, go off to Europe, or even China. He's that type. He'll leave and have adventures . . .

He glances at me. "Did you want—Ginnie! Are you all right?"

I blink, confused, then feel wetness overflow from my eyes and trickle down my face. I'm crying.

"What is it?" he asks.

I shake my head.

"Come on." He stands and puts his hand on my shoulder. "I'll take you home."

I shake my head again. What home?

"Come on."

His arm tentatively circling my shoulders, he leads me

away. I glance apologetically at Mrs. Weber, but she only pats my arm as we pass her, murmuring something about it being all right. I can't think of what will be all right, but I nod.

Outside, Kris starts across the street, but I drop down to sit on the curb. He sits beside me and again lays his arm across my shoulders. I've managed to stop the sobs that push against my chest. Tears have dried on my face, and my eyes burn.

"You okay?" he asks.

I hesitate, not certain how my voice will come out. "No." It's hoarse and painful.

"Is it . . . is it your folks?"

"You've got a great family."

He seems to understand. "We're not that great. If Ian and Aileen aren't fighting with each other, they're getting into trouble. Cara'll wander around the house not talking to anyone for days. Alta used to eat more dinners at friends' houses than at home, and Eli's hardly ever around anymore. It's like he's saying to Mom and Dad, 'I don't need you anymore.'"

I almost say he doesn't. But then I remember what Grandma said the second night I was there, talking about my parents, my mother getting jobs. "You young people today think you grow up so fast, leave home when you're eighteen and that's that, you'll never need your parents again. But that's not how it works. You never stop needing your parents."

Do Mom and Dad know that, know that I need them? Now, sitting here on this curb in Pittsburgh, the wet-wool-blanket air wrapped around me, I wonder if I could ever admit I need them. If I would ever have to. Isn't part of growing up growing away? Aren't I supposed to be forming a life separate from theirs? The ties between my mother and grandmother are still strong enough for Mom to chafe against them, and I tell myself that won't happen to me. Once I leave, I'll keep a clear distance between us. I'll change the mother-daughter relationship to one between two independent adults.

An odd pleasure and lightness fills me at the thought. Independent, separate. I see now that their dismantling of the Ryan home simply means that it's time for me to stop needing it.

A challenge, I think. Like driving the car too fast on dark roads. Take control and move the vehicle where you want, solely responsible for the trip.

"Kris," I say. My voice is still rough, and I take a few deep breaths to smooth it. "Kris, do you want to go someplace? I can't drive, but maybe we could walk . . . someplace?"

He nods. "Sure. There's the Friendly's at the bottom of the street. We could walk there and get dessert."

I stand up. "Let me just go tell Grandma."

F I F T E E N

Sunday night I dream about Grandma. She has moved from her big white house to a bungalow secluded at the end of a flat, narrow street. An overgrown privet hedge lines her walkway, and when I arrive in a neighbor's blue car, I tell her I'll clip the hedge for her.

Inside, her home is a mess, dirty plates and half-empty teacups scattered around a living room too full of furniture and books. I cannot believe she let it get like this, then remind myself that she is old.

I go away that night with the neighbor, a heavyset woman who wears flowered dresses, and come back the next morning. Grandma is waiting on the long porch for me, and she asks me inside. She walks swiftly to the door, her heels clicking on the porch's wood floor. Inside, the house is immaculate. Did she stay up all night to clean? But she looks rested and strong, as she was when I was a child, all quickness and energy and laughter.

I wake up before I can ask her how she grew young again. Hot, bright sunlight pierces through the long sheer curtains over the eastern window. I dress quickly and hurry downstairs to see her.

She is at the dining-room table, eating toast and drinking coffee. She smiles at me, then tilts her head in surprise as I kiss her cheek good morning. Her skin is still soft and fresh, her eyes clear and snapping. But comparing her to the Grandma in my dream, I see her skin has sunk beneath her cheekbones and drawn tight across her jaw, giving her the hawkish look I've seen in photographs of her mother and other ancestors. All tiny women with wide blue eyes and features that age hones to an unyielding sharpness.

I tell her I dreamed about her, and that she lived in a small house, somewhere far out of the city.

She laughs. "I would never move from here. Why, I've lived here for more than thirty years. Your mother tells me sometimes that the house is too big for me, and that I should move to Philadelphia to be closer to all of you. But this is her home too." She shakes her head sharply, and in her stubborn independence she's ten years younger. "Oh no, I wouldn't ever move."

Remembering the cluttered bungalow in my dream, I glance into the living room. It's clean, yet also a bit messy. Her *Gourmet* magazines are scattered on the sofa, and if I open her desk I'll find letters and bills tossed haphazardly in there.

"Speaking of Mom," I say, "I thought I'd call her this morning."

Grandma's mouth purses. "She won't be home. She has another job."

"Huh? Since when?"

"Since yesterday. I called her last night and she told me." Grandma's voice rises. "She's working at that vegetable place—Applebaum's?—as a checkout clerk."

"Appleton's," I correct her, swallowing a snort of part laughter, part embarrassment. The picture of my mother elegantly enjoying her solitude—I'd envisioned her in white, reclining on the sofa, cigarette in one hand, glass of white wine in the other; something out of *The Great Gatsby*—breaks apart. A checkout clerk is a far cry from real estate, but perhaps the lack of responsibility appeals to her.

"Well, that's interesting," I continue. "How come you called her?"

"Why, to talk. This is a terribly difficult time for your mother, being alone like this. Not that it will last," she adds confidently. "Of *course* your parents won't divorce. But they need to talk it out with someone who's objective."

Objective? I think. Hardly. And I realize Grandma and I haven't talked about Mom and Dad and the separation. Could it be because she won't acknowledge that this is serious, that it could mean divorce? Is that notion so appalling, she can't even consider it?

"Your mother and I had a nice chat," she goes on. "I *know* she misses your father, although she wouldn't say—"

A quick knock on the door interrupts her. This early in the day, I figure it must be Kris and slide off my chair. "I'll get it."

The inner door stands open to the cooler morning air, and through the screen door I see Diane on our porch, dragging anxiously on a cigarette and staring off toward a neighbor's house. Just as I am about to speak, she turns to the door. Her expression startles me, thin, tight mouth and panicked eyes.

"Thank God," she says. Dropping the cigarette to the porch, she grinds it out with her shoe, then looks at me and stoops to pick up the butt. She jams it into her tight jeans pocket.

"Diane, what's wrong?" I open the door to step outside, but she slips into the house instead. Shit. Now I'll have to introduce her to Grandma. She is dressed in her tough-girl clothes—a black tank top and white jeans. Her eyes looked bruised with heavy black liner beneath them. Her eyelashes are clumped with black mascara. "What's wrong?" I ask again, standing between her and Grandma.

"I saw Larry last night. My mom said I'm allowed out now, so I arranged to meet him." She glances past me into the dining room and lowers her voice. "We . . . uh, you know . . . and then he told me he was breaking up with me and wanted the ring he'd given me back."

God. That's a thousand times worse than what Denny did to me. "I'm sorry, Diane."

"Ginnie," Grandma calls. "Won't you introduce your friend to me?"

Shit again. I give Diane a What can I do? look and lead her into the dining room. "Grandma, this is Diane

LaSalle. Diane, this is my grandmother, Charlotte Alcott."

"Hi, Mrs. Alcott," Diane says politely. "Ginnie's been telling me how great it is to be spending the summer with you."

Grandma takes her time, inspecting Diane's flyaway hair and dramatic makeup, her provocative clothes, the silver bracelets that decorate one arm from her wrist halfway to her elbow. "It's very nice to meet you, Diane," she says at last, well-mannered to the bitter end. "Why don't you girls go into the garden to talk? I'm sure you'd like some privacy."

I lead Diane through the kitchen and out into the backyard. We walk down the stone steps and sit on the bottom one. "So tell me what happened."

Diane takes a deep breath. "You got any cigarettes? I smoked my last one on the way over here."

"There's some in my room."

"I need one real bad."

I dash up the steps and into the house. "Gotta get some Kleenex," I tell Grandma, and am halfway up the stairs before she calls that there's a box down there. I shove cigarettes and matches in my shorts pocket, grab a handful of tissues, and run back down. Grandma raises her brows as I race past.

Diane is wandering around the garden, checking out the pansies and snapdragons I planted when I first got here.

"What's this?" she asks, running a finger across the gently curved top of a white flower.

"It's a wildflower called Queen Anne's lace."

"It's real pretty."

I nod. "Most people call it a weed, but it's my favorite. Here."

She takes the cigarettes from me. "Thanks. Virginia Slims? I thought you smoked Kents."

"I changed my mind."

She lights the cigarette and draws in deeply. "God, that's good." She looks at me. "Do you think I'm addicted to these things?"

I stare at her for a moment, then laugh. My laughter angers her and she scowls. Then a smile cracks her tight mouth.

"Pretty funny, huh," she says, "since I practically chain-smoke."

"Hmm." I swallow a few last giggles.

"Do you want to hear about Larry?"

That sobers me, but I see the panic has left her eyes. She looks more sad than pained, and I wonder if she's been preparing for this since the night of the reckless driving. It's just too bad he used her like that first. We sit back down on the step, and she starts talking as I light a cigarette.

"I'm still not allowed to see him, you know, so I had to lie to my mother. I told her I was going out with Cheryl." Diane sneers. "I can't believe she bought that. I mean, Christ, why would I go out with *Cheryl* the first night I'm un-grounded?

"Anyhow, I walked over to a friend's house and called Larry at this other guy's house." She turns to me. "We had to do it like that, 'cause if Larry's mother knew I'd called, she'd tell my mother and all hell would break loose."

I nod.

"So he drove over and picked me up and we went out to this place. You know, where we always go to park."

Denny and I always went to a small wooded area at the end of my street. Without wanting to, I remember the feel of him lying on top of me, his hand up my shirt as he tried to coax me to unzip my jeans. My body flushes with heat at just the memory, and an insistent prickling quivers between my legs. I look away from Diane, embarrassed.

"And well, you know," she goes on, picking at the maroon polish on an index fingernail, "as soon as he stops the car he's all over me, telling me how much he missed me. He's already got his pants undone and my hand on him and I just couldn't stop him."

She pauses. I remain silent, staring at the Queen Anne's lace as I puff on my cigarette. I'm still thinking of Denny, of his disappointment, then frustration, then anger when I would give in a little more each night, but stop long before he wanted to.

"So what happened?" I finally ask.

Diane lifts her face to the sun, tossing her hair back, and takes one last long drag on the cigarette. "I let him do it. I thought we should wait since, you know, it'd been so long since we'd seen each other. But . . . he just wouldn't listen when I kept saying no."

A shiver shakes my shoulders, ripples down my spine. Denny always stopped. Maybe not immediately, but he did stop.

132

"Then what?" I whisper.

She lights another cigarette. Her hands are shaking. "He took me home. Well, not right to the house. He left me off a block away. We sat there for a minute and then he said that he thought we should see other people, that being apart these past weeks had made him think that we were too young to get all wrapped up in one other person."

"I'm sorry, Diane."

"Yeah." She stabs the cigarette into the stone step, crushing the ember and scattering ash and unburned tobacco. "The jerk. The goddamn fucking jerk."

"What are you gonna to do?"

"Do?" She looks up. The tears have leaked from the corners of her eyes; mascara and liner creep down her cheeks. "What do you mean, what am I gonna do? What can I do?"

I shrug. "Start dating someone else."

She laughs. "Who? No one's around in the summer. Most of the guys I know are jerks anyway."

"What about Steve?" She gazes blankly at me. "You know, the guy driving the other car the night we . . . uh, went cruising."

"Yeah, I remember that night," she says sarcastically.

"Well, Steve seems like a nice guy."

She shakes her head. "He's real smart, in all the top classes and stuff. He'd never ask me out."

"So why don't you ask him?"

"Forget it."

"Why not?"

She frowns at me. "Would you do it? Would you ask a guy out?"

133

"Sure," I lie. "If I liked him well enough."

"What if he said no?"

"I'd be no worse off."

She laughs shortly. "What if he tells everybody?"

That would be awful, and I have no answer.

"See?" she says. "Look, what about that guy Kris? Would you ask him out?"

Anxiety punches my stomach. Not because he'd say no. I'm sure he'd say yes. But it would mean a real date; it would mean I saw him as a boyfriend, as someone who could have more than that quick kiss in the garage. I think of his big hands at the ends of those long bony arms, think of them touching me. I think of his mouth, wondering if he knows how to French-kiss. My breath catches at the image of us lying in the backseat of Grandpa's Dodge.

Trying to look cool and impassive, I say to Diane, "I'll ask him out if you'll ask Steve out."

She tilts her head to study me out of the corner of her eye. It's an effective look, making me feel young and ungainly. But those black tear streaks lessen the effect.

"All right," she says. "But you've got to go first. And if he says no, the deal's off."

"No way." I stub out my cigarette and stand. "We both call."

"All right," she says, standing and brushing off her seat. "This is a crazy idea, you know."

I grin. "Yeah. But don't you feel . . . I don't know, more in control or something?"

She rolls her eyes. "You're real weird."

"I've been told that."

134

S I X T E E N

The phone on the desk in the upstairs hall has a long cord, and I carry it and the phone book into my bedroom. The vanity's too cluttered to set the phone on, so I sweep aside a couple of books, several stray necklaces, and a framed picture of my mother when she was fourteen. Diane is staring around the room, from the bed to the vanity, from the stacks of books on the floor to the clothes heaped on the spindly white chair.

"Wow, this is it?" she says. "It's so small."

No kidding, I think. "It's just for the summer. It's not so bad."

"And look at all these books." She glances at me. "You look like the type who reads a lot."

"I know."

I sit cross-legged on my bed, phone book in my lap. Diane perches on the edge. Finding the Webers' number, I dial quickly, before I can think about what I'm doing. As the phone starts to ring and my stomach starts to hurt, as if I badly need to go to the bathroom, I remind myself that this is just Kris. I can do this. Still, I hope he's not home, hope this is one of the days he's gone with Eli to work on someone's yard. The phone is picked up and I realize I've forgotten how to breathe.

"Hello?" It's Kris.

"Hi. Um . . . how ya doin'?"

"Fine. How are you?"

"Fine." Diane is giving me hurry-up signals. I steady my breathing and rush on. "Would you like to go out tonight?"

"I can't." He sounds sorry that he has to say no, but he doesn't sound surprised I've asked. "We've got company for dinner tonight and tomorrow night. Wednesday would be all right."

"Great." I guess he doesn't understand I'm asking him for a *date*. That's fine. "How about a movie?"

As he says "Sure," Diane leans over and covers the mouthpiece. "No. Tell him you want to take him to dinner."

"No!" I whisper.

"Do it or I won't call Steve."

She moves back and I glare at her.

"Ginnie?" Kris asks. "Are you there?"

"Yes, I'm here. Uh . . ." My heartbeat flutters like a panicked butterfly's wings, and communication between my brain and vocal chords lapses momentarily. "Do you want to go out to dinner?" I ask at last.

He doesn't answer, and I picture him blinking rapidly, his face taking on that irritatingly earnest expression it gets when he's trying to figure something out.

"Dinner?" he repeats. "Well, all right. Where were you thinking of?"

"Uh . . ."

"How about the Country Squire?" he goes on. "I've eaten there a couple of times. They've got some Italian food like lasagna, and hamburgers and fish. The food's good, and it's not very expensive."

"Great!" I say quickly. I've got to get off the phone before my heart pounds right out of my chest. "How about six o'clock?"

"Sure. I'll . . . uh, see you then."

"Right. 'Bye."

I hang up quick, not waiting to hear his good-bye. "Okay?" I say to Diane.

"Hey, you've got guts. That was pretty good."

I manage to laugh as the fear of passing out fades with the nervousness. "Thanks." I push the phone book toward her. "Your turn."

She flips through the book to find Steve's number, saying he may not be home, that he works at Burger King.

"Call him."

She checks the number four times while dialing, then silently counts the rings, plucking at my sheet. She jumps suddenly, her eyes widening, and says, "Hello." Her voice is shaky, so she clears her throat and repeats herself. "Hello. Is Steve there?"

137

I lean close, gesturing for her to let me listen. She pulls the phone a little away from her ear. ". . . is Steve," I hear him say.

"Oh, uh . . . Hi, Steve. This is Diane. Diane LaSalle."

"Hey, Diane. How are you? I heard your parents sent you to the Arctic Circle."

She laughs roughly. "Not quite. But I'm allowed out now. And . . . and . . ."

I nudge her. "Just say it fast. It's easier."

But Steve is speaking already. "I heard about you and Larry, too. I'm sorry."

"Yeah, well. I guess I know how important I was to him."

"I guess so."

Another nudge from me and she suddenly says, "Would you go to the movies sometime with me?"

"What?"

Not cool, Steve. Diane's mouth trembles and I feel stupid, putting her up to this right after her creep of a boyfriend dumped her. I almost grab the phone away, but she turns from me, pressing the receiver tight to her ear.

"Dumb idea, I know," she says. "I just . . . You're a pretty neat guy and, well, you're a lot nicer than the jerks I usually hang out with. And I thought . . ."

She is silent for a minute, her eyes squeezed shut as she listens to him. I'm frantic to know what he's saying, but she won't even look at me.

At last she opens her eyes, wiping at the tears and smearing her mascara. "Well, sure," she says. Another pause, then, "No, I'm not allowed to drive. We could . . ."

One more pause, and then, "Okay, that's great. I'll be ready. Yeah, 'bye."

She hangs up the phone and slides off the bed onto the floor. She drops her head into her hands, then throws it back and laughs. "Oh God, I don't believe it!" She twists and looks up at me. "He's taking me out Thursday night! Can you believe it?"

I bounce off the bed. "All right! You did it."

"Yeah." She scrambles to her feet. "Let's go someplace to celebrate. Let's go to Lenny's. We can play the jukebox and smoke up a storm."

Not my first choice of places to go. I'd prefer a smoky Parisian café, with soulful blues being played and Diane and me, sophisticated and irresistible, sitting at a tiny round table drinking whiskey, cigarettes dangling from our fingers. But we're underage, and in Pittsburgh, and it's only eleven in the morning.

We go to Lenny's.

Diane calls the next night and again Wednesday afternoon, alternately exhilarated and terrified about her date with Steve.

"No one knows but you," she tells me Wednesday. "You know, that I'm going out with him."

"Why not?" I ask.

"Oh God, everyone would give me a hard time. He's not . . . you know . . ."

"Cool like Larry." I don't mean to be blunt, but anxiety about my own date, less than three hours away, has dulled my sympathy for Diane. She's got a date with a nice, good-looking guy. What's she complaining about?

"So you haven't told Barbara?"

"Christ, no. She'd laugh her head off and then go tell everybody."

"She sounds like a great friend, Diane."

"Hey, she is. She's had a rough time of it. You know, her parents were divorced when she was nine and now she lives with her mother and stepfather and two half brothers. She can't stand her stepfather. I guess he drinks a lot and he's always telling her mother that she did a lousy job raising her."

"Oh." That arouses my sympathy. It doesn't forgive Barbara's cruelty, but it helps explain it. "That sounds pretty awful."

"Yeah. And you've only seen the hard side of her. She doesn't let people get close, but once she does, she's a really good friend."

"I believe you. But if she's a really good friend, why would she laugh at you for going out with Steve?"

"She wouldn't," Diane says quickly. "I was just saying that. But she wouldn't understand. I mean, the guys she dates, they're . . ."

I think of her sly smile that first day at Lenny's, when she asked the boy to take her for a drive. "I know what you mean."

We're silent for a moment, then I say, "I didn't tell you, but my parents separated this summer. I found out last week."

"Shit. You're kidding. God, that's terrible. Is that why they sent you here?"

"That's what my mother said. They wanted to see if they could work things out."

"Is one of them having an affair?"

I stiffen. What a stupid idea. Why would they? "No."

Still, I remember last summer, Dad going out at night, saying, "It'll be all right. . . . I'll explain. . . . I love you. . . ."

"No," I say again; then, "Mom says it's because they've changed, that they're angry with each other all the time and no longer want the same thing."

Diane laughs. "Shit, my parents have always been angry at each other. Hey, I'm sorry. I don't mean to make fun of it. So . . . you think they're gonna get a divorce?"

"I don't know. No one's said so. I guess this is just a trial separation."

"Yeah," she says, but I wonder if she knows any better than I do what that means. "Jesus, that's rough, Ginnie. I'm sorry. But you know, it's their life. You've just got to let them do what they want and not let it screw up your own life. You know, you don't owe them anything."

I half laugh; her words remind me of another conversation. "Not according to a friend of mine. I went to her birthday party the day after the last day of school, and she told me that because she owed her parents everything, she had to do what they saw as best."

"That's pretty stupid."

"She's one of the smartest girls in the school and could go to any college she wanted to, so I asked her where she was thinking of applying. She told me"—I imitate my friend's soft, earnest voice— " 'Only to colleges in the area so I can live at home.' "

"I asked her why, and she said, 'Because that's what my father wants.' She said he'd done so much for her, bringing her up, clothing her, feeding her. I told her parents are supposed to do that. Children don't *owe* them anything. She said children owe their parents everything."

"God," Diane mutters. "That girl's crazy. I'm with you, Ginnie. Parents do their duty and that's it. They knew what they were getting into. I mean, you should see my mom with her parents. Grandpa will give her this shit about how she should be doing more for them, that after all the years they took care of her, she should take care of them now, and Mom snaps back about how they never gave her anything. I mean, they just go at it all the time."

"You never get free, do you?" I say.

"Of what?"

"Your parents. The whole family. I mean, even if you leave home and never come back, you've still got a family."

Diane's silent for a minute. I expect her to deny it, to say that she'll cut all ties with her mother any day now. Instead she says, "I guess you're right. Maybe that's good. A home to go back to. You know?"

"I know. But what—"

I started to ask, But what if I don't have a home to go back to? Will I be all right? I can't think about that now.

"I have to go, Diane. I don't know what I'm going to wear tonight."

"Right. Hey, are you okay?"

"Yeah. I'm fine."

SEVENTEEN

Half a dozen tops, three pairs of pants, and two skirts lie scattered across my bed by the time I'm ready for my date. I've already lied to Grandma about it, saying Kris asked me out rather than the other way around. She would be shocked if she knew I'd called him. Bad enough she's expecting us to fall in love; worse if she thinks I'm not acting like a lady.

The only difficulty was when I asked her for the car. With great conviction I told her Kris couldn't use either of his parents' cars, and we were just going to the shopping center where the movie theater was, and we wouldn't be out late, and . . . and . . .

"It's fine," she said at last. I imagined knowing Kris would be in the car was the heaviest weight in my favor.

At quarter to six I go downstairs and present myself to

her. She is pleased by my choice of clothes. The last time she saw me go out on a date was when she was visiting over Easter. I wore faded jeans, a tight red top, and a cast-off denim jacket of my brother's. I stuffed a few dollars into a pocket, waved good-bye to her and my parents, and raced outside as Denny's motorcycle roared down the street.

I have to put my makeup on in the car. Grandma doesn't approve of makeup, saying it ruins a girl's face and makes her look "fast." I take the makeup out of the purse Grandma gave me for Christmas two years ago. I've hardly used it. Purses are too much of a pain; I prefer jackets, like that denim one of Tom's, with deep pockets.

I twist the rearview mirror down so I can see myself and sweep on the bronze shadow Diane convinced me to buy when we went shopping the day we called Kris and Steve. Oh God, too much. A gruesome streak of dark brown stains my lid. I rub at it with a tissue, smearing it down the corner of my eye.

I curse, then wet the tissue, clean it all off, and try again. Lighter this time, better. I don't bother with the blush Diane made me buy, but lightly run the lipstick across my mouth. It looks garish, but I don't wipe it off.

It's a few minutes past six now. I'm late. Grandma's probably wondering why the car's still in the garage and will come out any second to see if I'm all right.

I start the car and speed out of the driveway, then across the street, stopping in front of Kris's house. Grandma would kill me if she heard me honking the horn, but I'm not about to go to the door and ask for him. I wait, hoping he's been watching for me. After less than a minute he pushes open the screen door and steps outside.

144

He's wearing nice clothes too, chinos and a cotton shirt. I feel like we're playing dress-up, and pull the skirt of my sundress down over my knees.

"Hi," he says as he gets into the car.

I say hi back and take my foot off the brake.

It's a short drive to the Country Squire, but we can't think of anything to say. The restaurant looks fancy from the outside, and inside the formal red-and-gold carpet unnerves me. He said this place was cheap.

"Smoking or nonsmoking?" the hostess asks.

"Smoking," I say quickly.

I ignore the look Kris gives me and follow the hostess to the back of the restaurant.

The booths and tables reassure me. They're plastic. So are the menus. And the prices are cheap.

I smile at Kris. "This looks great."

"It's not bad. I've eaten here a few times." He studies the menu. "The hamburgers are good. So's the lasagna."

I nod and decide on spaghetti. Putting the menu aside, I ask, "Will it really bother you if I smoke?"

"No, it's all right. I mean, they're your—"

"I know, I know. They're my lungs." I pull cigarettes and matches from my purse. "You know, I'm not addicted to these things. I don't ever have cravings for them. I just smoke them because . . ."

I consider the cigarette as I light it, wondering why I do smoke. The three cigarettes I smoked in the garden after talking to Diane irritated my throat, as if a cat had scraped its claws across it, and I hate the tobacco stench that clings to my hair and fingers.

"You smoke them because . . ." Kris says.

I shrug. "Gives me something to do."

He leaves it at that, and the waitress comes to take our order. Kris asks for a hamburger, well done.

"I like your dress," he says as the waitress leaves.

I glance down at myself. The sleeveless cotton sundress, with a ribbed bodice and high waist, is not something I would have bought for myself. Mom gave it to me a few days before I left Philadelphia. She must have meant it as a peace offering, because she never buys me clothes.

"This is the first time I've worn it. I just wish they didn't have the air conditioning on so high." Goose bumps rise on my bare arms, and I hope that, with all the ribbing, Kris can't tell that my nipples are tightening with cold.

"You should have brought a sweater," he says.

"You sound like my grandmother," I snap.

He looks down, running a finger along the pattern in the paper place mat. "Sorry," he mutters. His finger traces the cartoonlike flowers, then he clenches his hand into a fist and stares at me. "Why do you make it so difficult to talk to you?"

I freeze, cigarette poised over the ashtray, mouth open, forgetting to exhale. Smoke clogs my throat. Coughing roughly, I grab my water glass. When the fit is over, I stare back at him.

"What do you mean, I'm difficult to talk to? You're the one who's difficult to talk to. Always going on about these boring books you're reading, and why I shouldn't smoke, and why I should be nice to my parents, as if I'm some kind of child who doesn't know how to act."

My voice has risen, and a few other diners glance our way. I lean forward, pressing against the table, and whisper, "I swear you think you're better than me, and it's some act of charity that you'll even be seen with me."

His Adam's apple works up and down as he swallows. He won't look me in the face; his gaze flutters around, over my shoulder, up at the ceiling, back down to the table. "Ginnie," he says in a tight voice, "that's not true. I . . . ."

His gaze is fixed, eyes wide, and I look down. My dress gapes away from my body, revealing my breasts. I snap back up straight, heat soaring into my face. We stare at each other, embarrassed.

"It's okay," he says.

What's okay? My breasts?

"Look, Ginnie, I like you. It's just that you get so defensive sometimes."

"What do you mean?"

"I don't know. As if you're always angry about something. You just . . ." He shrugs. "You won't let me be your friend."

"You've had a rough summer," he goes on when I'm silent. "With Denny breaking up with you and your parents separating."

"So?"

"See? You get defensive if I even mention any of that."

"Well what do you expect me to do?" My voice rises again.

"If you talked—"

"Here you go, folks," the waitress interrupts. She sets down Kris's hamburger and fries, then my plate of spaghetti and a basket of garlic bread. "Enjoy your meal."

"This looks good," I say, not letting Kris talk again. "Is your hamburger cooked enough? My mom always makes hamburgers so thick, the outside is burned and the inside is still raw. That's why I like McDonald's hamburgers better. They're so thin, they get cooked the whole way through."

Kris says nothing and pours ketchup over his fries.

The spaghetti is awful, the noodles soft and tasteless, the sauce thin and oniony, and the meatballs so mealy, they must be three-quarters bread crumbs. I can barely choke down a few bites. Kris finishes his hamburger and fries and glances around as if expecting more food to materialize.

"Do you want some dessert?" I ask him.

"Do you?"

I look down at the remains of my dinner. "Not here."

"We could go to Denny's again."

I smile, envisioning an enormous hot fudge sundae. "Yeah. Let's get the check and go."

The waitress brings the check and clucks over my unfinished meal as she whisks the plates away. The total is more than I expected, but I have enough money. My hot fudge sundae is downgraded to just a dish of ice cream, though.

I see Kris pulling out his wallet and say, "No. I'm paying."

"You don't have to. I can pay my share."

"I asked you. I'll pay."

He shrugs, starts to speak, then shrugs again. He shrugs a lot, lifting those narrow shoulders up toward his ears. The gesture bugs me, and I remind myself of other irritating habits of his as I count out my money.

"Dessert's on me," Kris says as we slide into a booth at Denny's.

I don't argue. "Then I'll have a hot fudge sundae."

His brows rise. "You're that hungry?"

"Kris." I lean forward, careful to keep one hand over my chest, and whisper, "That spaghetti was awful."

"Really? I'm sorry. Everything I've ever had there has been good."

"Just don't ever order their spaghetti."

He still looks morose. "I thought you weren't eating because I'd upset you."

"Well, you did upset me. I mean, I don't know what you mean about my being defensive and hard to talk to." His words seem insulting now, twisting painfully inside me. "You really don't think I'm a good friend?"

"No," he says quickly. "I mean, yes, you are." He stares up at the ceiling. "I told you I like you. You're just prickly. I can't . . . say the things I want to say to you."

Sweat breaks out on my palms again. Pressed to the table, I can feel my heart pounding against its hard edge. "Say things like what?"

He shrugs. "I don't know. I want—want to go out with you, do different things with you."

"Like boyfriend-girlfriend?"

He nods.

We sit motionless for a minute, he staring out the window, me staring at him and wondering what it'll be like to kiss him. Then he glances at me and reaches across the table to take my hand. My sweaty hand. I nearly pull pack, but his hand is hot and moist too. Maybe they'll just stick together, I think, and laugh.

He lets go as if I've burned him.

"No, no," I say, taking his hand back. "I wasn't

laughing at you. I was . . . I was just laughing."

His fingers carefully tighten around mine. "You have a weird sense of humor."

"I know. You're a little strange yourself."

He nods. "I know."

When the waitress comes we swiftly let go of each other. She takes our order and leaves, but we don't hold hands again. Kris plays with the yellow plastic salt shaker. I consider smoking another cigarette, but my throat's still raw. I think of all the cilia down there, the ones I saw in a biology movie in eighth grade, looking like the soft, tiny tentacles of some sea creature, fluttering as they try to move the smoke along and keep my throat and lungs clean. I'm killing them, I think, those cute little cilia.

Kris dumps some salt onto the table. "When do you think you'll go back to Philadelphia?"

I pull the cigarettes from my purse. "Soon, maybe. I don't know." A month ago the summer yawned in front of me like an endless black tunnel. Now I've got a friend and maybe a boyfriend. What's back in Philadelphia? A house.

I picture the house, brick with colonial-green shutters. They looked better when they were black. The floors are wooden, and familiar creaks accompany you as you walk along the halls, down the stairs, across the living room. Three bedrooms upstairs, and Dad's tiny den.

My parents' bedroom is always neat, the bed always made. But is it like that now, with only one person there? Does Mom make the bed since she's alone? Does she forget to empty the ashtrays? Does she make a whole dinner for herself, or just eat frozen ones? Does she watch TV in the evening? Does she stay up late? Do the floors still creak?

If there's no one around to hear, do floors creak when you walk across them?

I look at Kris, the unlit cigarette between my fingers. "I wonder if she wants me to come back. My mother, I mean. I wonder if she's lonely, or if she's happier alone, and I'd just be intruding."

"You're her daughter," he says. "Of course she wants you to come home."

"You don't know." I light the cigarette. "She's had people around her for twenty years. Maybe she's glad there's no one there now."

"Well, maybe she likes it some, but I'm sure she misses you and . . . your father."

"Maybe."

Back out in the hot night, we stand indecisively beside the white Dodge.

"Can I drive?" Kris asks.

I hesitate, wondering about insurance, wondering if I want to give up control. But I'd seem petty and scared if I refused, so I hand him the keys and walk around to the passenger side.

Sitting without either a seat belt or steering wheel, I feel insecure on the wide, long seat. My fingers keep tying the strap of my purse into a knot, and my leg muscles tighten as I press down on an imaginary accelerator and brake. I don't know where Kris is going, for he's driving through a foreign part of the suburbs. The streets are dark, with large houses spread farther apart than on Grandma's street, and set back on wide lawns.

Kris slows the car, then stops near the end of a street,

out of the circle of light from a streetlamp, between two driveways. He turns off the radio, the lights, the engine. The silence and stillness enclose us.

"Ginnie?" He slides out from behind the wheel. "Would it be all right if I kissed you?"

My fingers clench around my purse. "Yes."

I set the purse on the floor, beside my feet, and turn to him. The dimness shadows his face, darkens his eyes. He could be anyone. He touches my shoulder, my cheek, as if to be sure I'm really there. He lowers his head slowly, and I tense. I remember to close my eyes, to tilt my head back.

His mouth brushes mine like a kiss in a dream. He pulls away, but before my eyes open he kisses me again, rubbing his lips back and forth across mine, as if to strike sparks. I catch my breath, wondering why I want this so much.

I rest my hands on his shoulders, and his own find my waist. He grabs my dress, bunching it in his fists.

We stay like that for several minutes, barely touching, barely kissing until my neck aches from not moving.

"Kris," I whisper. "My neck."

I ease back and roll my head from side to side. "Here." Sliding into the corner of the seat, I curl my legs up. "Like this."

I hold out my arms and he moves close. Tentatively, he places his hands at my waist and bends down. When his lips touch mine, I open my mouth. He shudders, his hands clutching me.

"It's all right," I tell him.

He nods and kisses me again. His lips part against mine; the tip of his tongue touches mine. We don't move, held rigid by this new feel, this new taste. Then his grip on me eases and his tongue slips farther into my mouth. The anxiety's that's cramped my stomach for hours eases, and I sigh and hold on to him, happy he is kissing me.

When we shift positions again, he pulls me onto his lap, his bony legs hard beneath me. I am taller now, and lean down to kiss him. His face is no longer shadowed, though the night has darkened his hair. His eyes are half closed as he looks up at me. I stroke a finger across his skin, where his cheekbone and jaw jut out in sharp angles, wondering if one day he'll be handsome.

Impatiently, he pulls my head down. He is bold now, taking control. His hand hovers over my breast, then touches it.

I stiffen. "No." The thundering of my heart, the heat scorching my cheeks, the wetness between my legs, frighten me.

"Why not?" he whispers, trying to kiss me again.

"It's too soon."

"All right."

I let him kiss me, and he keeps his hands on my back, rubbing them up and down, finding the bare skin of my shoulders and neck. His touch there is dangerous, and once more I pull back.

"I don't want you to leave yet," he says.

"Leave where?" I ask, confused.

"Back to Philadelphia. Stay here until school starts."

I am silent, then kiss him. "I gotta get home."

E I G H T E E N

'm not gonna go with Steve tonight," Diane an-
nounces.

I switch the phone to my other ear. "What? Why
not?"

"I'm just not. I don't want to. I bet he didn't mean it
anyhow. I bet he isn't even going to show up."

"Come on, Diane. I don't believe that. He doesn't
seem like the type who would do something like that."

"Just goes to show what you know. He's already got a
girlfriend, you know."

"He does?" I sit up straight on my bed. "Who is she?"

"Just this girl. She's not here. Her folks always go away
for the summer. I think they're in Germany or someplace
this year. I guess Steve just dates around while she's
gone."

"I guess." I think back to the night of the reckless driving, remembering that girl Debbie storming out of his car and screaming at him about how crazy she must have been to want to go out with him. He'd looked surprised, and I'd thought it was because no girl had ever wanted to date him before. But it was because he already had a girlfriend.

"Has he dated anyone else this summer?" I ask Diane.

"I don't know. I don't really hang out with his crowd, you know." I hear a sucking sound. She's smoking. It's like talking to my mother, all these strange pauses in conversation. "You know why I think he asked me out?"

You asked him out, I silently correct her. "Why?"

"Because . . ." Long deep drag, then she whispers, "Because he knows about me and Larry."

"Well, yes. I mean, you didn't date anyone else while you were going with Larry, right?"

"Not that," she says sharply. "Not that we'd broken up. That we . . . you know."

"Oh. Oh!" Shit. He wouldn't really ask her out for that, would he? "Hey, you wouldn't. Would you?"

"No." She puffs on the cigarette, and I can picture her, squinting against the smoke, hands trembling, then the thumb heading for a chip of color left on a fingernail. "I don't think so."

"Diane! You can't. If you do . . ."

"Yeah?"

Tough girl again. "Diane, listen. If you do, he'll tell other guys, and that's all anyone will ever want from you."

"So? What's the big deal? It's not like I'm gonna fall in

love with every guy I do it with. And it's fun, you know. You should try it sometime."

Not if I panic when Kris touches my breast.

She goes on. "It's not this big deal, like everyone makes it out to be. It's just fun. You don't have to be in love and married to the guy. Everyone does it just for the fun of it."

When I'm silent, Diane sighs impatiently. "Look, I know you don't approve, but just don't hand me any of your puritan shit. You can save yourself for marriage, but you're gonna miss out on a lot of fun."

"I didn't say I'd save myself for marriage. But at least I'm going to save myself for love."

"I loved Larry!"

"You're only seventeen, Diane. That's too young to be in love."

"Tell me you weren't in love with Denny."

"I wasn't! That's why I wouldn't have sex with him. I didn't love him."

"That's a bunch of shit. You probably—"

"Forget it, Diane. You go ahead and sleep with Steve. I'm sure it'll make him very happy. Just don't forget to use a condom. It's not worth getting pregnant or getting AIDS."

I hang up. Sitting absolutely still, I try to blank out the entire conversation. No, the fight. We had a fight. I never fight with my friends, not like that. Not cursing at each other, yelling. She'll never talk to me again. I'm sure of it.

Downstairs someone knocks on the front door. I hear Grandma say, "Oh, good morning, Kris. Won't you come in? Ginnie! Kris is here."

When I reach the living room, hands stuck in my shorts pockets, he's sitting on the couch, like he was that first day. Still too skinny and gawky, his long arms and big hands just waiting to knock something over, he doesn't snatch my breath away like Mel Gibson. Yet as he smiles and stands, I don't think he's gawky anymore. I know his body now. I've felt it against mine. He's kissed me and touched me.

"Hi." I don't look at him, afraid Grandma will see in my eyes what happened last night.

"Hi," he says. "You doing anything?"

"I was going to weed the garden. Do you want to help?"

He shrugs. "Sure."

We start toward the back door, but Grandma says, "Ginnie. Aren't you going to offer Kris anything to eat or drink?"

I look at him. He shakes his head.

"It's okay, Grandma. We'll get something later."

Outside, I suck in a breath of the hot, moist air. "The dog days of summer. And I thought it was hot three weeks ago."

"This is unusual. We're supposed to get thunderstorms this afternoon."

"Good." I walk to the garage, and he follows. "You know," I say, "summer heat might not be so bad if we were someplace else. Like Italy or Greece. I always think of that saying, 'Mad dogs and Englishmen go out in the midday sun,' and I picture some sunny piazza in Italy, where you can sit at an outdoor café and drink iced coffee and watch the world go by."

Seeing he's staring at me, I haul open the garage door and mutter, "Don't listen to me. I've probably got heat stroke."

"No," he says, walking into the dim garage with me. "I like that, a piazza in Italy. You've got a great imagination. And you should do that someday, sit in a café in Rome, or Venice even, and watch the world go by."

I laugh shortly. "Sure. Here, take these." I hand him the weeder and a spade, then grab the gardening gloves and Grandma's ancient straw hat. I plunk the hat on my head and start back toward the sunlight, but he takes my hand.

"Wait."

I turn. My heartbeat quickens; my breath catches in my throat. He tightens his hand around mine and moves closer.

"I'd like to take you to Italy," he says. "And anyplace else you want to go."

Something's wrong. I can't breathe. He bends his head, hesitates, then kisses me quickly, lightly. I can breathe again and step back.

"Right," I say. What were we talking about? "You . . . uh . . ."

I give up and leave the garage. He follows silently.

"I just talked to Diane," I say as I bend over a bed of flowers, plucking out the blades of grass.

Kris pulls up a flowering weed. "How is she?"

"Okay." She just thinks I'm a jerk. "You know, she's going out with Steve tonight."

"No, I didn't know. Who's Steve?"

"You remember." I glance at him. "He was the guy

driving the other car that night."

"Oh, him. So they're going out."

I can see he couldn't care less. Taking the weeder, I dig into the hard ground around a dandelion. How can I tell him about the fight?

"We had a fight."

"Who?" He walks over to me and sits on the ground. "You and Diane?"

"Yeah." I grab the dandelion and pull. The root breaks off a few inches down.

"What about?"

I attack another dandelion. "Sex."

"What?"

I sit and face him. "Sex. She thinks it's okay to do it with just anyone. She thinks I'm a prude." I stab the weeder into the ground. "Do you think that? I mean, do you think it's okay to sleep with whoever you want?"

He draws his legs up, curving his arms around them. "I don't know. I guess if you don't care, if you're just doing it for fun and don't expect it to mean anything, it's all right. But . . . I wouldn't want to do it like that."

"No?" I start working on the dandelion again. "Denny wanted to sleep with me."

"I figured that."

I snap my head up. "You did?"

"Sure." He tugs at the grass, tearing it. "It was some of the things you said about him. And guys usually want it more than girls."

"Do you want it? I mean, would you sleep with me?"

We stare at each other, my mouth open as I try to take the words back. I didn't mean to say them, not make it

sound like I'm asking him to. I'm just trying to understand. I turn away, standing and walking over to the yellow day lilies. Plucking off the dead blossoms, I hear a
soft sound behind me, then feel him standing at my back.

"Not if I didn't love you," he says.

I keep breaking off the dead flowers and throwing
them behind the lilies, back by the wall that separates our
yard from the neighbors'. We stand together until only
the budding and blossoming lilies are left.

"Ginnie, do you want to . . . ?"

I shake my head wildly. The hat flies off. He picks it
up and holds it out to me.

"It's not because I don't like you," I say quietly, staring
at the hat, at his hand. "It's just . . ."

He sets the hat on my head. "I know."

"No you don't!" I cry suddenly. "You don't. I want to
do it. I want to do everything! I want to be ten years older
and—and on my own and making my own decisions. I
want to have all these things figured out. Even just be
three years older and in college, and go out for drinks
with friends, and stay up late talking about what we're
studying, and—" I stalk across the yard. "Just be on my
own!" I yell back at him.

He watches me, uncertain and wary. He likes me, I
think. Even if he tells me I'm prickly and defensive and
hard to talk to, that I don't appreciate my grandmother
and read trashy novels, he still likes me.

I smile timidly at him. "I'm okay now. I didn't mean
to yell."

"It's all right." He walks over to me. "I know how you
feel. I feel like that too sometimes. That's why I said I'd

take you to Italy." His hands on my shoulders, he dips his head to see my face under the brim of the hat. "We can start planning for it. Say we'll go next summer. We can make plans, and maybe that'll make you feel better."

He's crazy. We can't plan for that. We're too young.

But I'll be eighteen next summer, out of high school and on my way to college. It's not so crazy. And it's not so far away.

I smile and nod. His hands creep around to my back and he eases me against him. I drop the hat and rest my head on his chest. I can hear his heart beating, faster and faster as he holds me.

N I N E T E E N

I call Diane right after dinner, but her mother tells me she's not there. I wonder if she broke the date with Steve, or if they just went to an early movie.

Kris can't go out. More company. His aunt and uncle from Cleveland, along with their three kids, are there for a long weekend visit.

After washing the dinner dishes, I roam around the living room, fumbling tunes on the piano with one hand, staring out the screen door as a few cars go by, reading one of my favorite fairy tales from the collection of children's stories on the shelves by the door.

At eight, an old Fred Astaire and Ginger Rogers movie comes on. Grandma and I watch it and agree that it's too bad they don't make movies like they used to. When it's over, we have our ice cream, then she takes her bath. I get into bed with my latest Lord Peter Wimsey mystery, *Busman's Honeymoon*. It's the last one with Harriet Vane, and I'm reading it slowly, dragging it out. They're married now and share a bed, but there's no description of their lovemaking.

Except for one paragraph, when he holds his hands out to her, and she thinks of how those hands touched her last night, before, behind, between . . .

I think of Kris's hands, imagine them caressing me. We're in the car. I'm on his lap and wearing the sundress. He slides the straps off my shoulders, off my arms, pushing the bodice down to my waist. He touches my breasts, lightly. I want him to kiss them and I grasp his head, urging it down—

I throw the book on the floor and roll over onto my stomach, forcing away the tingling between my legs. Is Diane doing it right now with Steve?

Friday morning I fill a bucket with ammonia and warm water, drag the hose around to the front of the house, and scrub the porch. I'm hosing off the last soapsuds and dirt when Kris strolls up the walk.

"Looks like fun," he says, keeping back from the spraying water.

"It's a blast, the most fun I've had all summer." I give the corners one last sweep with the water, then turn the hose off. "What are you up to today? Do you have to work?"

"No. Eli's taking the day off. My cousins and Mom, Ian, Aileen, and Cara are all going to the zoo. Would you like to go?"

I look warily at him. Zoos are great—if a bunch of kids aren't complaining and screaming and dragging you off everywhere. "Are you going?"

"Only if you want to."

"I'd just as soon dig pota—"

I stop when the phone rings inside. Grandma answers it, and we hear her say, "Oh, hello, Diane. Would you like to speak with Ginnie?" Her shadow leans over the couch as she calls to me out the open window. "It's for you."

"Come on in," I say to Kris as I drop the hose.

We tiptoe across the wet porch. Inside I tell Grandma I'll take the call upstairs.

I carry the phone into my bedroom, where I sit on my bed. Kris perches on the white vanity chair and scans the books stacked on the floor.

"What's up?" I ask Diane.

"Oh, gee, nothing. I was just calling to talk about the weather."

I laugh. "All right. Did you go out with him?"

"Yeah."

"And . . . ?"

Kris has swiveled on the chair so his back is to me, but I'm sure he's listening.

"It was okay. We went to see *Terminator 2*, which was pretty cool. Afterward, we went out to get pizza. I really wanted a hamburger instead, but he said after working at Burger King for three years, he's sick of hamburgers."

"I'll bet. Did he pay?"

"He sure did. Paid for everything. Hey, I never asked about your date. How did it go?"

"All right. What did you do after the pizza?"

164

She doesn't answer for a moment. I close my eyes. They did it. I know they did. I tell myself it's not right, even as I wish I could do it too.

"He brought me home," she says.

"What!"

"I thought you'd like that. He brought me home. Didn't even try to kiss me, or hold my hand at the movies or anything. Shit, why'd he want to go out with me?"

I start to giggle. "I don't know, Diane. Maybe he likes you."

"Huh? Well, yeah, but . . ."

"Not everyone kisses on the first date, you know."

Kris looks up at that. He's been reading *Gone with the Wind,* but closes it and grins. A keen awareness of him pierces me, like a shivery sliver of ice. We share something now, something private and secret. We're linked.

"I always kiss on first dates," Diane is saying, "unless the guy is a real jerk. What about you? Did you and Kris kiss?"

"Yes, we did."

"Did what?" he asks.

"Yeah? How was it?"

"Not bad."

"What?" he asks.

He stands and walks over to me. I scoot back to the corner of the bed, cradling the phone protectively.

"Did he French you?" Diane asks.

"Diane! That's crude."

"Does that mean he did or didn't?"

He's kneeling on the bed now, leaning close. I'm starting to giggle. "What do you think?" I ask Diane.

"From the looks of him, I'd say he didn't. But the way you're talking, I'd say—"

"Stop!"

His hands, curved menacingly, move toward my ticklish waist. I twist away, yelping as his fingers dance across my middle.

"What's going on, Ginnie?" Diane asks. "Is he there with you?"

"Yes," I gasp, vaulting for the end of the bed.

"You're kidding? Your grandmother lets him up in your bedroom with you?"

"Why not?" I'm smacking his hands away, laughing. He's laughing, too, and I love the sound.

"Christ, my mother would just as soon shoot a guy as let him up here in my bedroom."

"Grandma thinks Kris is a gentleman." I laugh at him. "Hah. Little does she know."

He pretends to behave, then his hand shoots out and he tickles me again.

"Stop!" I cry, jumping off the bed and nearly snapping the phone cord.

"Ginnie!" Grandma calls from downstairs. "Are you still on the phone?"

Kris and I stop instantly, staring at each other. "I'm just getting off, Grandma."

"Then maybe you and Kris should come down."

"I gotta go, Diane," I mutter into the phone.

"Yeah, I heard. Look, I'm heading for the pool in about an hour. You going today?"

"Hang on." I ask Kris if he wants to go. He nods, and I tell Diane we'll see her there.

Hanging up, I unwind the phone cord from around me. "We better get downstairs." I grin at him. "I bet that's the first time you ever got in trouble with my grandmother."

Everyone's at the pool. I ask Kris if he wants to sit with Diane and her friends and, typically, he says no.

"Diane's okay," he says, "but I don't really like anyone else. They all smoke too much."

I glance over at the group, agreeing silently. "We'll compromise then," I say. "How about over there, behind that woman with the three kids?"

He looks toward the empty spot on the far side of Diane and company, close enough so we can wave to each other, far enough so we can ignore each other. "Okay," he says, and walks along the edge of the pool to it.

I follow, smiling and waving at Diane. She calls back, "Hey, Ginnie!" and scrambles to her feet. When she reaches me she leans close, dragging her feet to slow me. "I think Steve's coming today," she whispers.

"Really? He told you that?"

"Sort of. I mean, he asked last night if I was going to be here, and when I said maybe he said maybe he'd see me."

"Great. You really like him, huh?"

"Who wouldn't? I mean, he's cute, he's got his own car, he's got money to spend. . . ."

I laugh. "Diane, you're supposed to like the *person*."

"Really?" We've reached Kris, and she smiles down at him. "Hey, Kris."

He nods. "Hello, Diane."

She looks back at me. "Let me know if you see him."

"I will."

"You got any cigarettes? I'm almost out."

I go blank for a moment, trying to remember if I remembered them. I changed into shorts and a T-shirt, got my bathing suit and towel, found a book to read. . . . I shake my head. "No, I forgot mine."

"Oh. Oh, well. See ya." She flips a hand and walks away.

I spread out my towel. Kris watches me smooth the bumps before sitting down, then he reaches over and runs a finger up my arm.

"I meant to ask you," he says, "if you got into trouble Wednesday night for getting in so late."

I shiver, from his caress and from memories of what we did Wednesday night. "It was still before midnight." I open my book—a hardcover I got from the library, *Touch Not the Cat* by Mary Stewart—and carefully tuck the bookmark in the back. "Grandma just asked if we'd had a nice time."

"She was still up?"

"Sure." I look down at the book, pretending I'm reading already. "She always stays up late. She usually doesn't take her bath until ten or so, and she's always up early, like around five or six."

"That's all the sleep she needs?"

"She's told me she's never needed more than six hours."

"How old is your grandmother?"

"Kris." I look up with exasperation. "I'm trying to read."

"Oh. Sorry."

We both read for about five minutes, then he says, "Ginnie?"

"Yes?"

"Does your mother still have that job at the vegetable stand?"

I nod. Her job doesn't embarrass me anymore. It's distinctive, having a mother who works as a checkout clerk and is proud of it. "She called last Tuesday night and told me about it. She says she feels a sense of power, weighing people's vegetables and then taking their money. She's getting to know the customers, too. She says sometimes these young couples come in, and they ask her how long they should cook the corn on the cob, or how to tell if a cantaloupe is ripe. It makes her feel important, she says, as if . . . as if she's learned a few worthwhile things in twenty years of marriage."

Kris sits up. "She said that to you?"

"Sure."

"That's a rotten thing to say. Was her marriage only good for cooking vegetables? What about you and your brother?"

"What about us? We're fine."

"There you go again."

"What?"

"Being defensive."

"Give it a rest, Kris. I'm not being defensive. Just see how you deal with it if your parents ever break up."

"That's the point, Ginnie. You're not dealing with it. You're pretending nothing has happened, that you'll go home and everything will be like it was."

Anger steams through me, and I don't even look at him. Who's he telling me how I'm feeling? "You been reading Freud again, Kris?" I ask nastily. "Getting into psychoanalysis?"

"No," he mumbles. He hangs his head, tearing the grass. "I don't know why I keep saying things that make you mad."

He looks up, right at me. His eyes are wide, his face vulnerable. He's so easy to hurt, so easy that I'm tempted to do just that. But he kissed me. He sat me on his lap and held me and touched my bare skin. I can't keep hurting him, can't keep pushing him away. If I do, then I can't have what I had two nights ago.

"It's all right," I say. "I'm not mad anymore." Leaning over, I kiss his cheek. I half expect him to grab me like Denny would, to roll me onto my back and kiss me and tickle me. Instead he squeezes his eyes shut like a little boy, then opens them and kisses me on the lips. It feels nice. Maybe I *will* stay until school starts.

We go back to our reading, and half an hour later a wet hand touches the hot, bare skin of my back. I yelp and roll over. Diane stands above me, dripping on me.

"Hey!" I exclaim.

"Sorry." She moves back and drips on Kris instead. "He's here!" she whispers, kneeling down. "As soon as I got out of the pool I saw him. He's with a couple of guys over on the other side."

I start to sit up, but she pushes me back. "Don't look! He'll see you."

"So? It's not like you just have a crush on him and you

don't want him to know. You went out with him last night."

"Yeah, but . . ." She glances over her shoulder, then sits on a corner of my towel. "What if he doesn't want the guys he's with to know about me?"

I consider that, then shrug. "It wouldn't hurt just to wave at him, would it?"

Chewing on her lower lip, she stares at her hands. She must have done her nails yesterday in honor of her date, because the polish isn't chipped at all. She runs one thumbnail across the other, as if in frustration. When she looks up, she turns to Kris.

"What do you think I should do?"

He and I are both startled that she's asked him, and he blinks rapidly.

"I don't know," he mumbles, not quite looking at her.

"But you're a guy," she persists. "I mean, what if it was Ginnie on the other side of the pool? Would you want her to wave at you, or would you mind if she came over and talked to you?"

"It's not the same situation," he says slowly, and I want to hit him.

"Can't you pretend?" I ask. "Use your imagination?"

He flinches at my sharp tone, and I sigh. Why is this so hard?

"I think," he says after a moment, "that if I liked a girl and she came over to talk to me, I'd be flattered."

"But what if you had all your friends around?" Diane asks.

He stares across the pool. Does he have friends? I

wonder. Since I came to Pittsburgh, he seems to have spent all of his free time with me, and I've never heard him mention any friends. My irritation of a minute ago softens.

He shrugs. "I don't know, Diane. I still think I'd be flattered."

She says nothing, sneaking looks across the pool. Kris starts reading again and I lie back down, trying to think of something she could do to get Steve's attention that would seem perfectly natural. I could pretend to drown and she could rescue me, hauling me to that side of the pool and calling to Steve to help her. But the lifeguard would probably get involved and I'd look stupid.

"Hey." I sit up. "Let's race."

"What?" Diane asks.

"You and I will race back and forth across the width of the pool three times. We'll end up on Steve's side of the pool and our racing will probably have gotten his attention."

"I'm not that good a swimmer," she says doubtfully.

"We'll go slow then. Come on."

I stand up, and so does Kris. "Ginnie." He takes my hand. "You might get sick again. Remember what your mother said."

Diane stands as well. "What?"

I grimace. "After I wrote her about getting sick, she told me I might have a hiatal hernia—whatever that means. They're hereditary, and I guess they run in my dad's family. He's got one and has the same problem when he swims too much." Diane's looking dubious, so I add, "We'll go slow. I'll be okay."

Kris doesn't appear reassured, but he does let go of my hand.

"Come on, Diane."

We walk to the pool and slide into the water near the deep end, across from Steve. I shiver at the sudden coolness after the heat of the air, and allow myself to sink, wetting my head. I bob back up and look at Diane. She's got a death grip on the side of the pool.

"Ready?"

She nods.

"I'll give you a head start. Just swim as fast as you can."

"I'll probably drown," she mutters.

"Then he can rescue you. Go on."

She hesitates for nearly a minute, then pushes away from the side, straightening her body and slicing through the water. She's faster than I expected, and I take off after her.

I feel nothing but water and the stretching of muscles, hear nothing but splashing and the strange echoing underwater noises. When I turn my head for a breath, I glimpse purple-blue sky above me and vague colors around me, and the rippling edge of the water. Then back down at the bottom of the pool, cool green and wavering.

We're even as we start the third lap, and my lungs are burning. I hear my own gasping as I snag breaths of air, and worry that Kris and Diane were right. I'm going to get sick. I push harder, wanting to finish before whatever happened last time happens again, and surge in front of her just a few feet from the edge. I win.

We hang on to the side of the pool, panting and half laughing.

"You're a good swimmer," I say between gasps.

"Thanks. But you won."

"Yeah. And I'm beat. I hope you don't mind if we walk back."

She winks and starts to push herself out.

"Wait." I slide closer. "Your mascara is starting to run."

"Shit." She slips back into the water and frantically rubs beneath her eyes. "This stuff's supposed to be water-proof."

"It's just not race-proof. There's a little more in that corner."

She gets it all and we turn to climb out of the pool. Steve is standing above us.

"Hi, Ginnie," he says to me, then hunkers down in front of Diane. "Hey, there," he says softly.

"Hi."

She can't quite meet his eyes, and he smiles at her. It's a great smile. I'm wondering if I should just creep away, when he says, "You two want a hand out of there?"

"Sure," Diane says quickly.

He grasps her arms and helps her up. I clamber out by myself. Once Diane is standing, Steve lets go of her, but doesn't move away.

"Thanks for the race," I say to Diane. "See ya."

Neither seems to mind that I walk away.

"Are you okay?" Kris asks as I ease down onto my towel.

"Uh," I say, lying on my back, one hand pressed to my stomach. "I'll be all right."

"Does it hurt?"

"Just a little. Not as bad as the other time." I can feel the muscles knotting, but without the intense cramping pain of before. "I'll be all right," I say again, and close my eyes.

I sense him hovering over me, then his hand covers mine. Remembering how last time I wanted him to touch me, I look up. He's leaning close, his eyes wide and un-blinking.

"I don't want you to hurt," he whispers.

Pain radiates from my stomach to my chest, tingles of warning. I don't tell him, certain that if I lie perfectly still, they'll fade.

"I'm okay," I whisper back.

He is motionless for a moment, then he bends down and touches his lips to mine. "Okay," he says. "But tell me . . ."

"I'll tell you." My fingers tighten around his as a small, sharp cramp races through me. He frowns with concern.

"Ginnie . . ."

"Just hold my hand, okay?"

"Okay."

T W E N T Y

Kris and I walk home slowly, holding hands and talking. I didn't get sick at the pool, yet the cramps kept me lying on my back for more than twenty minutes. He stayed and read my Mary Stewart book to me.

When I felt better, I sat up and looked across the pool. Diane was still with Steve, sitting apart from his friends. They shared one towel, their bare shoulders touching. Diane was laughing, tossing her head so her hair swung about her, and I hoped she appreciated my suffering.

I don't get to Grandma's until nearly six. She's ready to serve a macaroni and cheese casserole, but tells me my mother called and wants me to call her right back.

My stomach does the same nauseating somersault it did at the pool. There's no reason to think anything's wrong. But not much has been right this summer.

Mom answers on the first ring. "Is that you, Ginnie?"

"It's me." I plunk down on my bed. "What's up?"

"I just wanted to talk. How are things out there?"

"Pretty hot."

"Mmm, this has been a brutal summer. I bet you've been spending a lot of time at the pool. Do you go with friends?"

"Mostly Kris from across the street."

"Oh? I thought you didn't like him."

"No, he's a nice guy." I'm willing to give her that much.

"Well, that's good. The summer hasn't turned out as badly as you expected."

How the hell can she say that? Didn't her summer turn out badly? Or was she hoping Dad would leave? Is she hoping I'm not coming back?

"Ginnie, I'm sorry. I shouldn't have said that. I'm just glad that your time in Pittsburgh hasn't been terrible. When I talked to Grandma earlier, she said that you seemed quite happy. You weren't even that upset about Denny anymore."

I consider what else Grandma would have said. Certainly she would have told Mom about my date with Kris. So much for protecting my new secrets.

"No, I'm not upset about Denny anymore." I stare out the window. The sky is still blue, though paler now as the sun sinks. Mom asks when I'm thinking of coming back, and I don't answer for a minute.

"I don't have to be back until Labor Day."

She doesn't speak. The silence lasts for another

minute. When she does talk again, her voice is softer, weaker even. I can't picture the face to go with this voice. I can't picture a weakness in her.

"Ginnie, I'd like you to come back. I'm . . ." A deep breath. "I'm lonely. This house creaks when there's only one person here."

"Why don't you ask Dad to come back?"

It's hurtful, but I want that. I want her to explain. I want her to tell me he did something terrible, or that she loves another man, anything that would be clear-cut and easy to judge. Something more than boredom or "irreconcilable differences."

"Your father doesn't want to come back. But he misses you too," she adds quickly. "He wants to see you."

"I'll check my calendar," I mutter.

"Ginnie, I know all of this has been hard on you. It's been hard on your father and me too. I think it might be easier if you were here, though, and we could all talk."

"Talk about what?" My hand is clenched around the phone, and I yell into it, "When have we ever talked about anything? Nobody talked to me about this! You just went ahead and did it, got rid of me and then got rid of each other. You want to know why I eavesdrop all the time? Because you never talk to me. I'm just trying to find out what's going on."

"Ginnie, that's not true. We talk to you."

"Oh, yeah. 'Are you coming home for dinner? Why don't you ever go over to Karen's house anymore? Why did you drop out of volleyball?' Real important stuff."

"Those things are important. Everything about you is important to me."

"Right. Everything except how I feel about things."

"Ginnie." Her voice is strong again, and I can see her face now, the tightness at the corners of her mouth, the level stare beneath the level brows. "That is not true. Both your father and I care about you, about how you feel. But you've pushed us away. You've made it very difficult for us to talk to you. Communication is a two-way street."

Bullshit, I think, bunching the sheet up in my fist. The burden is on them. They're older, the parents. If they can't figure out how to talk to me, why should I bother figuring out how to talk to them?

That's unfair, but I'm tired of fair. "Never mind, Mom. I just want . . ."

"I know, Ginnie. You just want to be grown-up and not have parents anymore. At least, not parents you live with and have to deal with all the time. But you've got another year to go before you leave for college, and I don't want to fight you every day until then."

She knows that? I never said any of that to her, never truly thought it through myself until a week ago. "How did you know that?"

She laughs a little. "When you've watched a person grow up, there's not much you can't figure out about her. I knew when you were two years old that you were always going to be impatient and want to be older. You would imitate your brother and the other older kids, pretending you were as big as they were. And you are very grown-up. But . . ."

"But I'm still only seventeen and I still live at home."

She pauses. "Yes. And maybe you won't believe this, but I want this last year with you. I don't mind so much

179

your brother going off to college and hardly ever coming back. He was always more of a loner than you, never needing to be with me and talk with me as much. But I know I'm going to miss watching you grow up once you're gone. You've changed even just this summer, and I'm sorry I didn't get to see that. It's wonderful to watch your children become adults, adults you can respect and love."

Startled by this new view of parenthood, I slide off the bed and walk over to the window. I never considered that she was eager to see me become an adult. I figured she'd want it parent and child all the way.

"It's okay if you want to stay until Labor Day. You're right. You really don't need to be here until school starts."

"Well, I guess I can call Dad and ask when he'd want to come out and get me. Unless," I add hurriedly, "you want to come out."

"We'll see. I don't work the same schedule every week at Appleton's. I'd have to see when I could get time off. But it would be nice to have a visit with Mother."

"She'd like that. So . . . um . . ." I twist the cord around my finger. "Let me know."

"I will. And you stay in touch. Write me another letter. I like getting them."

"All right. And Mom? Can you give me Dad's address?"

July 25

Dear Dad,

I never really answered that last little letter I got from you, and since I can't just write to you and Mom at the same time now, I figured I should write you.

I keep the letter chatty—telling him that I've made friends with a girl named Diane and one of the Weber kids; that I went to see *Terminator 2* the other night. A little bit about Grandma, how she occupies herself with nearly nonstop letter writing and phone calling. I end by saying I don't know when I'll be coming home.

I seal the envelope, address it and stamp it, then write to Mom. I don't intend the letter to be any longer or any different, but the words flow out, filling a couple of pages before my hand cramps and I stop.

July 25

Dear Mom,

It's a really beautiful day today. Unbelievable. The sky is that perfect summer blue with just a few fluffy white clouds, and though it's hot, it's not insufferable. I'm sitting down in the garden writing this, and everything is blooming. The pansies have gotten enormous—they're fighting it out with the snapdragons for space—and the rosebushes just keep blooming and blooming. I pick flowers for the house almost every day. It's too bad Grandma really can't take care of the garden anymore. Sometimes when I'm out here weeding, she'll stand at the top of the steps and just watch. She says that's enough, but I can tell she misses it.

I have to confess that I wasn't entirely honest with you on the phone last week. About Kris, I mean. Actually we've had a couple of dates. It's a long story how it got started, but we've had a good time. I like him when he's not acting smarter than me, and he seems to like me too. We go to the movies, and then usually get some ice cream. I had dinner with his family one night too. I like them all, though that house must get even more crowded when everyone is home.

Have you heard anything from Tom? We got a letter from him yesterday. It was short, but he said he's having a good time, that it's a good group this year. No one's drowned yet, though when a canoe capsized last week, one of the guys in it hit his head and knocked himself out. A counselor dove in and got him, and gave him mouth-to-mouth. He was okay, and Tom said he got right back in the canoe and took off. Like me, when I kept being thrown by that bad-tempered horse at camp last summer. You know, I was the only girl who ever fell off, but then I always rode Squaw, and she was the only horse who would throw a rider. Don't ask me why I always chose to ride her. I guess it was the challenge each day, that this time I'd figure out how to stay on her back. Some days I did, and I got real good at landing on my feet and mounting without anyone helping me.

This is a long letter, and I feel as if I haven't even told you that much. I'm still up in the air about when I want to come back. I am having a good time here now, and Kris wouldn't mind if I stayed until Labor Day.

Take care.

No, I think, rereading the last paragraph, Kris wouldn't mind at all. When we took a walk yesterday, he asked me when my school started.

"The day after Labor Day," I told him, but I didn't want to talk about that. We were walking with our arms around each other, and I kept tightening my hold on him, keeping his hip against mine, thinking about the night before. He'd come over after dinner for ice cream, and then Grandma had gone upstairs for her bath, leaving us alone in the living room.

We sat on the couch talking, but he was more interested in caressing my arm. The light strokes sent tingles racing up to my shoulder, my neck. When I turned to face him, he kissed me. More daring than before, he bit my neck, ran his tongue up and down it and into my ear. He squeezed my breasts, and I pinched my legs together to keep from squirming, bit my lip to keep from gasping.

For one moment, as we lay in the dark room, the night air wafting over us, the couch cushions as soft as water beneath my back, his body felt as natural and familiar to me as my own. I held him, trying to hold on to the feeling, but it slipped away. The memory lingered, though, bringing me closer to him than I'd ever been to Denny.

"You can stay then," Kris went on, "through Labor Day weekend?"

I hadn't considered staying that long, and dragged my thoughts back from wondering how something physical could also be emotional.

"I think I should leave before then," I said. "I mean, I've got to get ready for school and stuff."

"What do you need to do?"

"Buy new notebooks and pens. Some new clothes. Things like that."

"You could do that in an afternoon. You could do that here." He stopped walking, tightening his grasp on me to stop me, too. "It's already the end of July. Why don't you stay for the whole month of August, till Labor Day?"

I stared at the sidewalk, scuffing some pebbles. "It'll depend on my parents, you know, when someone can come out and get me. My dad hates traveling over holidays, because the traffic's always so bad. And you know the Pennsylvania Turnpike can get pretty mobbed."

"Ginnie."

He swung me about and held me. My arms slipped around his waist, my hands flat against his narrow back. His heart beat fast and hard against my chest, and I could hear his quick breathing in my ear.

"Ginnie," he said again, and I realized what he wanted to say. Words crowded against my own closed lips, and I pushed my face into his shoulder, stifling them. I couldn't love him. I was too young, and I was going back to Philadelphia.

He rubbed his cheek against my head and hugged me harder, squeezing breath from me. I didn't try to free myself. In that tight embrace, I felt what he couldn't say.

We stood in the hot sun for several minutes. I thought of nothing, only that his thin frame was strong; all my weight rested on him, and he supported me easily.

When his arms loosened and he leaned back, I looked up at him. He kissed me and said, "I feel very old right now."

I was puzzled, for I still felt too young.

"Never mind," he said, and we walked back to Grandma's.

TWENTY-ONE

Grandma wakes me up at six thirty Saturday morning. "Your mother's on the phone."

"What?" I mutter, pulling the sheet up over my bare shoulders.

"Your mother's on the phone. Hurry and get up. She wants to talk to you for a minute before she goes to work."

Why can't she wait until evening, I wonder. I wait for Grandma to leave so I can get out of bed, not wanting her to see me without clothes on. She stands over me, though, as if certain I'll go right back to sleep if she leaves. Rolling over, I tug the top sheet free and gather it around me. It trips me up twice as I shuffle to the desk in the hall. Grandma now disapproves of my taking the phone into my bedroom. She thinks I'm being secretive. I set the phone on the floor at the top of the stairs, sit down, and mumble into the receiver.

"Hello, Tallulah Bankhead," Mom says, dropping her own voice an octave.

I tighten the sheet across my breasts. "I was asleep."

"Sorry about waking you, but I wanted to talk to you and Grandma before I went to work about how you'll be getting home." She pauses, as if preparing herself for something momentous. And it is momentous. "Grandma would like to give you Grandpa's car."

"Huh?" Still sleepy, I'm sure what I heard is not what she said. "Grandpa's car?"

"Yes. You know Grandma has no use for it, and she's been thinking of selling it for months. But she told me how much you like it, and how much she likes to see you driving it. She doesn't want to sell it to strangers. So she wants you to have it."

"Grandpa's car? I'm getting Grandpa's car?" It's what I keep hearing, so I must be hearing right. "Are you kidding?"

Mom laughs. "No, I'm not kidding. So that's how you'll be getting home. You can either drive by yourself, or I'll fly out and spend a few days, then drive back with you."

Drive by myself, all the way to Philadelphia? Through those tunnels? I shake my head. Too much all at once. "Mom, I . . . uh . . ."

"Think about it, Ginnie. I know it's a big shock first thing in the morning. We can talk about it more tomorrow."

"Grandpa's car." The sleep-hoarseness has left my voice, and when I add, "Wow," enthusiasm breaks through.

"There, you're starting to sound more like yourself. Is it sinking in?"

"Yes." I picture myself wheeling that big white car into the high-school parking lot, impressive beside Denny's little motorcycle. "That's great, Mom. Thanks."

"Thank your grandmother. It was her idea. And think carefully about driving back by yourself. I think you can handle it, but if it makes you too apprehensive, it's no problem for me to come out.

"I've got to go, honey. I'll be late for work. Oh, it's nice to hear you and Kris are getting along so well."

"Hmm. Have a good day at work."

She laughs. "I always do."

I hang up and lean against the railing. Grandpa's car. I don't believe it.

I dress and race downstairs to thank Grandma, hugging her and laughing as she smiles and pretends it's no big thing.

First thing after breakfast, I run across the street to the Webers'. When Kris answers my rapid knocking, I blurt out, "I got Grandpa's car!"

"What?" He pushes open the screen door.

"Grandma's giving me Grandpa's car and I'm going to drive it back to Philadelphia!"

He steps out onto the porch and carefully closes the door behind him. "When are you going?"

The wariness in his eyes dampens my enthusiasm.

"Mom said I could stay until Labor Day," I say softly.

"Good," he says, but his voice is vague as he stares off toward my garage.

"Want to go for a drive?" I ask.

"I can't." He doesn't look at me. "Dad asked Eli and me to work in our yard this morning, mow it, clip the hedges. It'll take a few hours."

"Come over later, then."

He turns. His face is blank, his eyes dull, like an overcast sky without rain. I've seen that expression before, and privately call it his half-witted one. Now I understand that he's forcing away his sadness, all emotion. I brush my hand against his, then grab hold.

"I'm sorry," I whisper. "I don't want to leave you."

He stares down at the concrete steps, his shoulders hunched, his straight hair—which badly needs a cut— falling over his face. He's unattractive for a minute, and a part of me rejects him, wanting my boyfriend to look perfect all the time. But other parts of me . . . like him.

He jerks his head up; his eyes lighten with inspiration. "You could stay," he says quickly. "Transfer here and—"

"No. Not my senior year."

He nods. "I figured that. But . . . I could go to Philadelphia with you."

"What!"

"Not to stay. But drive there with you. Then I could fly back."

What a lousy idea. I've already decided I want to do this alone. I'll handle my fears of the tunnels when I get to them. For now I picture myself looking enigmatic and self-contained, driving in a big white car along the

Pennsylvania Turnpike. I can pretend it's a German Autobahn, or maybe a highway through France or Italy, and I'm an expatriate, a famous writer like Fitzgerald.

Kris's body is rigid. I try to imagine the two of us in the car. It might be fun, laughing and listening to the radio, talking about the people in the other cars. He could even help with the driving. Maybe.

"I could ask," I say finally. "Would your parents let you go?"

He shrugs. "I think so."

We stand awkwardly, hands held yet eyes shifting away. "Maybe," I say, "we could go to a movie tonight, get something to eat after that."

We both know what I mean. "After that" means "after dark," when we can drive someplace and park and kiss. He said the other day that we have a few more weeks together, which might sound long enough. But when I think that that means only three more Mondays, it's not very long at all.

"Okay," he says. "I'll check the paper. How about—"

"Yo, Kris!" Eli yells from inside. "Kiss Ginnie goodbye and get out into the backyard. We've got work to do."

Kris blushes, red blotching the tanned skin across his cheekbones. I giggle.

"I gotta go," he mutters, not looking at me as he turns to the door.

"Wait. Your brother said you're supposed to kiss me good-bye."

Almost panicking, he glances up and down the street, then across to Grandma's house. I wouldn't be surprised if she was watching out a living-room window, but I put my arms around his neck.

"Come on. People kiss on doorsteps all the time."

His hands flutter at my waist, then settle. The gleam of retaliation replaces the panic in his eyes. I suddenly see the danger in teasing a guy who's got six brothers and sisters. He knows how to get even. I press back, away from him, but his grip is too tight. He bends his body, curving it over mine, and kisses me. Not one of his swift, half-embarrassed kisses, but an open-mouthed, wet-tongued kiss. He holds my hips to his, and I feel his penis stir and harden. Frantic, I strain back against his strong grasp.

He releases me. His lips are moist, and he looks both surprised and satisfied. "Good-bye, Ginnie." He steps into the house. The door slams shut and he's gone beyond the screen. I stalk back across the street.

Diane isn't home, and I wander around the living room, wondering what to do with myself. Kris's kiss loosed a tantalizing wetness in me. Every few minutes I look at the clock and figure out how many hours there are until we can go to a movie and he can kiss me like that again. Grandma is paying bills at the dining-room table, apparently unaware of my restlessness. At last she carefully fixes a stamp to the last envelope and looks across the room at me.

"Do you need new clothes for school this year?"

"Not really," I answer. "I don't grow out of them like I did when I was ten." Actually, I'd love some new clothes, but not the ones Grandma would want to buy me.

She smiles and shifts her gaze, staring into the past once more. "I remember that darling little suit we got at

Horne's when you were in fifth grade. It had a gray wool jacket and that yellow-and-gray-plaid skirt. You looked so darling in it."

"Well, I don't wear suits to school anymore."

"Oh, I know." She straightens, affronted. "You wear those jeans all the time, and your brother's shirts."

"Not all the time. I've got some nice pants and shirts."

"Don't you ever wear skirts?"

"Oh, sometimes." Like maybe twice a semester. "Nobody dresses up much."

"A young woman," Grandma says, "should always dress nicely. You don't want to make yourself ugly.

"I think we should get you some nice clothes," she goes on. "Not just for school, but for evenings, too. After all, you're growing up and boys—*young men*—will want to take you out to nice restaurants and plays. Even the ballet."

"I suppose." Except that Kris will be here, and I can't think of a single guy in my whole high school I'd want to go out with.

"Well," she says, collecting the bills, "we'll go to Horne's after lunch, all right?"

"Sure." I look at the clock. Ten fifteen. Eight hours until I can see Kris.

Grandma and I spend more than two hours at Horne's. They are having a sale, and after loading up on stockings—never pantyhose—she picks out for herself a cotton jumper almost exactly the color of her eyes and a blouse to go with it. In the Misses department, she sends me into the dressing room with two summer dresses and one for fall, three skirts, and two blouses. I try everything on and model for her and the rather stern, gray-haired saleslady. The two women discuss what does and doesn't work while I quickly add up totals. Mom warned me before I left Philadelphia that if Grandma took me shopping, I wasn't to let her spend more than fifty dollars. A blouse and skirt alone cost sixty, and I can see she really likes one of the summer dresses, too.

When I'm all done dressing and undressing, and my hair is staticy from pulling clothes over my head, she insists we take a dress, the short, narrow black skirt and the longer navy one, and a cherry-colored blouse. I tell her it's too much. She laughs and hands her Horne's credit card to the saleslady. I argue and start to take the clothes back to the racks. She says my name—*Virginia*—and snatches the clothes from me, her nails catching my skin.

"If I can't buy clothes for my granddaughter," she whispers fiercely, "I don't know what good my money is."

"But Mom said," I plead. "You aren't supposed to spend this much."

Her eyes frost over and she lifts her sharp chin. "Your mother too often thinks she knows what's best for me. But she is my daughter and you are my granddaughter, and I won't have either of you telling me what I can and cannot do."

She's got a point, I decide, and give in.

When we return home, I toss the blue Horne's shopping bag behind my bedroom door, then pull it back out and empty it onto my bed. Clothes and tissue paper float down onto the white spread. Holding the black skirt up against myself, I look in the mirror. The skirt's so narrow, it's almost slinky, emphasizing my waist and hips. Not something I'd wear to school.

Pushing aside the other skirt and the blouse, I spread the dress out across the bed. Full-skirted and sleeveless, with a square neckline and buttons all the way down the front, it's as feminine as anything Grandma ever bought me. And there's nothing childish about it.

Fingering the stiff cotton, loving the crisp, fresh feel of it, I wonder if when I wear it, it will make me pretty.

Kris arrives while I'm washing the dinner dishes. He asks me if I want to see *Terminator 2* again. I say yes, and he tells me we'll have to leave in about ten minutes. Enough time to finish the dishes, if he helps dry.

I'm scrubbing the pot we cooked rice in when the phone rings. Grandma answers, laughing as she says, "Oh, hello, Richard."

"Shoot," I whisper to Kris. "It's my dad."

"Can you ask him to call you back tomorrow?"

I give him the look he so often gives me, the one that makes me feel like I have no brain. "Kris, when your folks have separated and you haven't seen your dad for a month, you don't tell him to call back tomorrow."

He shrugs, studying the plate he's slowly drying, as I leave the kitchen.

"Hi, Ginger," Dad says heartily. "How are you?"

"Good. Grandma and I went shopping today."

"Uh-oh. I bet she bought out the store."

"Just about. We kind of went over budget."

"Your grandmother has a tendency toward that. Did she make you buy skirts?"

"Two of them. And a dress."

"Good for her. You've got to show off those legs of yours, Ginnie. You can do a fashion show for me when you come back."

I start to speak, but can't think of what to say. How do we do this now? When do I see my father? Does he come to pick me up, like a date? Do I meet him someplace so Mom doesn't have to see him? Do I even tell her?

Dad understands my silence. "It's not that bad, Ginnie. Your mother and I talk to each other. This is only a trial separation, you understand. It doesn't mean that we'll get . . . that we'll never live together again."

The word's divorced, Dad. "Okay. Did she tell you about the car? Grandpa's car?"

"Yes." He's back to hearty. "That was very generous of your grandmother. Do you think you can handle driving back alone?"

"I think so. Although . . . maybe a friend of mine will come with me. Would that be all right?"

Grandma, leafing through a magazine and obviously listening, perks up. She tilts her head toward me as if to hear better.

"Who?" Dad asks.

"Kris. You know, the boy from across the street."

From the corner of my eye I see Kris standing in the dining-room archway, drying the rice pan. He winces when I call him "the boy from across the street."

"How would he get back home?" Dad asks.

"By plane."

"I see. Is there something going on between you two?"

"Da-ad."

"Well, your mother did mention him on the phone this morning. Something about a date you two had."

"Well, you know." I silently tell him that both Grandma and Kris are listening, but he doesn't get the message.

"What's he like?"

"You've met him, Dad."

"Have I? They've got so many kids over there, it's hard to keep them straight. Let's see. Kris, Kris . . . Oh, is he the tall boy, well-built, blond hair? He's in college, right?"

"No, that's Eli. Kris is the younger one."

"Younger? How young?"

I hesitate, wrapping the phone cord around a finger. "Sixteen."

"I see. Does he have a driver's license?"

"Of course he does."

"Don't get angry with me, Ginnie. I just want to make sure this is someone I trust driving all that way with my daughter."

"I don't think he's part of a gang."

Kris smiles at that, but Grandma stiffens.

"Look, Dad, he hasn't even talked with his parents about this, so it may not happen. I don't know when exactly I'm coming home either."

"Well, I suggest that if you're going to wait until Labor Day, you come home on that Sunday. There'll be much less traffic and much less chance of an accident."

I stare out the window as a bus roars past. "That's very encouraging, Dad."

"I'm just being realistic, dear. And I know the tunnels make you nervous."

"I can handle it!"

"I know you can. I wouldn't have agreed with your mother if I didn't. I just want you to understand that a six-hour drive across Pennsylvania is different from a joyride around the neighborhood."

"I know, Dad. Look, Kris and I are going to a movie."

"Is he there now?"

"Yes."

Dad chuckles. "Sorry about that, honey. I didn't mean to embarrass you by asking all those questions."

"It's okay."

"I love you."

"Right. 'Bye."

I hang up and look at my watch. "Do we still have time?" I ask Kris.

He nods. "I finished the dishes."

I grab the car keys off the piano. "Great. We're outta here, Grandma."

I kiss her cheek, and Kris and I sprint to the back door.

TWENTY-TWO

So what did your dad say?" Kris asks, as we share a banana split at Denny's.

"About you driving with me?"

He nods.

"I guess he thinks it's okay. Did you ask your parents?"

"No." He concentrates on cutting off a bite of banana without slopping melting ice cream onto the table. "I didn't think you liked the idea all that much."

My turn to concentrate. "I don't know. You took me by surprise. I just . . . Well, it's kind of a wild idea, you driving all the way across the state with me, then flying back here."

"I thought it would be fun."

He says this hesitantly, as if he's afraid I'll laugh at him.

"I think it would be too," I say.

He smiles. I forget the ice cream on my spoon, my mind overloading with memories of this morning's kiss on his front porch, and the kisses just now in the movie theater. I want to say, Let's forget this banana split and go someplace dark and private, but I haven't got the nerve.

"I'll ask my parents tomorrow," he says. "I don't think they'll mind."

I nod, though I didn't really hear what he said. The fantasies spinning through my mind take over. Will he get me into the backseat tonight? Will he take my shirt off? Will I let him touch my bare breasts? Will I let him touch me . . . there? Will he want me to touch him?

A shiver ripples my shoulders and tightens my nipples. I blame it on the ice cream.

"Ginnie?"

Forcing the fantasies aside, I focus on him. "What?"

He points at the table. "Your ice cream."

The whole blob has fallen off my spoon and onto the table. "Shit," I mutter, and pull napkins from the tin container to mop it up.

"Is something wrong?"

"No, nothing's wrong." I wad up the sticky napkins and shove them to the far end of the table.

"You know, I haven't seen you smoke all day yesterday or today."

I'd noticed that too. Ever since our first date, I've left my cigarettes in my bedroom. I don't forget them on purpose, but I don't miss them either. "I guess you're having a good influence on me."

He leans forward, sliding the banana split out of the

way. "I'm glad," he whispers. "I like kissing you better when you haven't been smoking."

"Oh." I rub my finger across a streak of ice cream on the table.

"Are you done?"

I nod.

"I'll go pay."

He gets up and starts across the restaurant to the cash register, pulling his wallet out. I watch him, trying to see him as a stranger. From the back, he looks good—if you like thin guys. With his long legs, he has an easy, loping stride, and his arms don't seem so gangly as they swing in rhythm. He stops at the register, leaning against the counter, his profile to me. I stare at his chest, remembering the feel of his heart beating inside it, then stare at his backside, remembering when we were walking yesterday and I slipped my hand into the back pocket of his shorts. He started, then smiled and put his arm around my waist, his big hand cupping my hip.

A waitress rings the bill into the register. He hands her money, and he doesn't smile and flirt with her the way Denny would. Denny flirted with all the girls, and I always worried that one day he'd just go off with one of them.

The waitress gives Kris his change. He walks back to me, and I study him from the front. His shoulders are too narrow, but I like his hips. Then, realizing he's watching me stare at him, I look away and wish I hadn't forgotten the damn cigarettes.

"You ready to go?" he asks.

"Yes."

I let him drive, and this time sit right next to him, my leg and shoulder against his. He takes me to the same neighborhood. As we cruise along the still streets, I notice other suspiciously parked cars, their windows almost all the way up and foggy.

"How'd you know about this place?" I ask.

He shrugs and pulls to the curb. "Eli told me."

"Really?"

"I guess it's the kind of thing big brothers tell little brothers."

"When did he tell you?"

He shuts off the lights and ignition and puts his arm around my shoulders. "Last Monday, when you asked me out."

"Oh." My heart is pounding hard, and I want to put him off for a while, hoping I'll calm down. "So you've never been here before. Before Wednesday, that is."

His brows furrow in a small frown. "You knew that. You're . . . you're the first girl I've dated."

"I am?"

"You knew that," he repeats, almost angrily.

"No I didn't. I mean, I thought I might be, but you never told me. Am I the first girl you ever kissed?"

He hesitates, then nods, staring out the windshield.

Not sure what's wrong, I slide closer and say, "I like kissing you."

"What about . . . what about Denny?"

"What about him?"

"I mean, he must have been a lot more experienced, a lot . . . "

From reading novels, I've learned a few things about men

and women. One, never say "I love you" for the first time right after making love. Two, never say "I love you" and then ask the man if he loves you. Three, never compare.

"I don't care about Denny," I whisper. "The creep broke up with me. Which is okay, because now that I'm going with you, I would have had to break up with him."

I might be stretching the truth there, but I don't let it bother me. I'm feeling romantic. I like what we're saying, the way we're sitting in the dark car. This is private, just between him and me, and I'm going to hoard all of these secrets. Secrets between men and women, I think, are part of growing up.

I brush my cheek against his shoulder, a signal that he should kiss me. He does. I twist to kiss his neck, taking little bites. His skin has a sharp taste, different from Denny's. I like it. Closing my eyes, trying to turn off my mind, I move my head down, following the open collar of his shirt. He draws in his breath, then one hand cups the back of my head while he unbuttons his shirt with the other. He guides me to his bare chest, sighing when I gingerly lick him.

"Ginnie," he whispers. "You too."

I sit up and look directly at him. He falters, then as meticulously as he dries himself off at the pool, he unbuttons my blouse. I slide it off, and he reaches behind me for the hooks of my bra.

"I'll do it," I say quickly, not wanting him to fumble with them.

I get them undone, then hang on to the bra for a moment, embarrassed and uncertain. He kisses my neck, my shoulder, my chest.

"Please, Ginnie."

I let him take the bra off. He touches me. His trembling fingers brush across one breast, and I feel the caress with my whole body. Shuddering, he slides his arm around me to urge me closer. I arch my back and our bare skin touches. Tremors vibrate through me at the sudden warmth and smoothness. He kisses me wildly as he searches for my breast again. He cups it, squeezes it. His breathing is hard and fast.

Little noises are pushing from my throat. I want something but I can't ask him. I try to tell him wordlessly, pressing my body upward and grasping his head, urging it downward. He understands. I shut my eyes as his mouth leaves mine, then gasp when it closes on my breast. He knows what to do. Instinct. He sucks on me, and a fierce heat clamps around me.

Did Denny ever do this to me, make me feel like this? I can't remember.

Kris's mouth leaves one breast to go to the other, and he grasps my right wrist. Slowly, he turns my hand and carries it down, down, between his thighs. He presses it against his hard penis. My mind blackens, my breathing stops. I'm going to faint, even as my fingers curve naturally around him.

"Ginnie, is that all right?"

"I don't know." A tiny sob of doubt catches my voice. I slip my other hand down his bony chest, then around his back. "Just kiss me."

He does, holding me tightly. My hand slides away, and he doesn't put it there again.

T W E N T Y - T H R E E

Mrs. Weber stops by after lunch on Wednesday with four pints of blueberries. "I'm sure you can use these," she says, as she hands me the cardboard containers. "Your grandmother tells me you make wonderful pies."

Not exactly true. "Grandma makes wonderful pies. I just help."

"That's not so," Grandma says, pushing herself out of her chair to join us. "You made the pumpkin pie last Christmas all by yourself."

"Well, pumpkin . . . pumpkin's easy."

I carry the berries out to the kitchen while Grandma and Mrs. Weber catch up on the neighborhood gossip. I've eaten half a cup of berries by the time Grandma joins me.

"How about a pie now," she says, "and blueberry muffins for breakfast."

I agree, and we push aside the catalogues, cut-out recipes, bits of glass serving pieces, and other assorted useless treasures that clutter the broad table in the kitchen. She makes pie dough while I make the batter for the muffins. While the muffins cook and the pie dough chills, she mixes the water, cornstarch, and sugar for the berries. Plump and sweet, they don't need much sugar. I keep a close eye on the muffins—the timer on the stove broke years ago, and she never bothered to buy another one—and she rolls out half the pie dough. Despite her arthritis, she wields the rolling pin nimbly.

"These are the best blueberries I've had in a long time," I say as I pull the muffin tin from the oven. "Where did Mrs. Weber get them?"

"She sometimes drives out to a farmers' market outside the city. They always have the best produce."

"A farmer's market. Sort of like where Mom works?"

Grandmas stiffens just a little. "I suppose," she says.

She folds the flat circle of dough in half and lays it into the bottom of the pie plate. It fits perfectly, of course. It doesn't crack or have an uneven edge that needs patching, like my crust always does. She sets the plate aside and gets the rest of the dough out of the refrigerator. "Here," she says. "You roll out the top."

Slowly, easily, I flatten the dough with the heel of my hand, working it into a rough circle. Then I dust flour on the rolling pin and set the pin to work. I use it too lightly, and Grandma curves her hands around mine and presses it into the dough. I nod and keep rolling, working from the center out, expanding the circle, easing the dough up from the table and circling it around, catching stray flour beneath it.

As I roll, Grandma pours the berries into the pie plate.

"How come Mom never learned to make pie dough?" I ask as she dots butter onto the berries.

"Your mother never *wanted* to learn," she says, resigned but, I'm sure, still regretful. "She much preferred playing baseball and basketball. She just didn't want to do what I did. She always tried to be like her father. He encouraged her, of course." Her high voice sharpens with disappointment in her husband and daughter.

She sprinkles cinnamon on top of the berries, then dabs water along the crust edge. "All ready," she says.

I've finished with the dough, and cut into it the design she taught me—two elongated S's with a few teardrop shapes beneath them. Folding the dough in half, I lift it. It stays in one piece, supple yet firm. The design is off center, but once the first slice is lifted out, no one will notice.

"Let's put it right into the oven," she says. "We'll have it for dessert tonight. Maybe you'd like to invite Kris over."

"Okay."

As she puts the pie in the oven, I gather the scraps of dough and divide them into two piles. One for eating and one for making a tart.

"See, Ginnie," Grandma says as she snitches a piece of dough. "You did fine with that."

"Hmm, well, maybe I just need more practice."

"Keep practicing then," she says lightly. "You know

what they say, the way to a man's heart . . ."

I turn to get myself some milk. "That seems . . . manipulative."

"Manipulative?" she echoes, as if she's never heard the word before.

"It's as if you're saying, don't worry about what I'm like as a person, just think of all the great food I can make you."

She laughs. "You're being silly, Ginnie. Of course it matters what kind of person you are. But it's important, too, that you know how to cook. After all, your husband's not going to want to eat out every night. It's fine when you're courting, but he'll love coming home to a house that's filled with the aroma of dinner cooking, a pie that you baked . . ." She sighs, as if she can smell the pie already.

"*He* comes home? Why can't *I* come home and *he's* made dinner?"

With a hard sweep of her hand, Grandma whisks flour off the table and into the metal wastebasket. "Why are you so . . . belligerent, Ginnie? I'm not saying that women shouldn't work. After all, I had a job before I married your grandfather. I had to give it up, of course, because during the Depression married women couldn't work and take a job away from a man or an unmarried woman. No, I think it's fine that women work, so long as it doesn't interfere with their families.

"You have to remember that, Ginnie. Your husband and children will be the most important part of your life, and if you do have a job, it should never overshadow them."

I drain my milk glass, rejecting the life she foresees for me. She's appalled that I'm looking at colleges that aren't within commuting distance of home, and I know she expects that after I graduate, I'll live at home until I marry. And marry young. And have children right away. I've heard her disdainful comments about women who put their careers ahead of starting a family; women who discover, when they do want a family, that they've waited too long.

I won't wait too long, I tell her silently. But there's so much more to this world than just a husband and children. So much to see. So much to learn. So much to do, alone.

Kris comes over around nine, and Grandma tells him I made the blueberry pie. I don't argue, since he demolishes his first piece, with ice cream, in about two minutes flat and wants another.

Rain falls heavily that night. There's no wind, so we leave the windows open. The pattering sounds of the rain hitting the bushes and the striped awnings over the porch and front windows are background music to the clinks of our forks and Grandma's voice. She's telling the story of the first pie she made for Grandpa. He helped her peel apples. He was a whiz at it, she says. On every one, he spiraled off a single long red twisting length of apple skin, never breaking the peel. She was very impressed.

After we've finished the pie and she has drained her teacup, she smiles at us and stands. "I'm going to go take my bath now. Ginnie, you don't mind cleaning up, do you?"

I shake my head, excited and nervous that she's leaving Kris and me alone again. I don't look at him but jump from my chair, carrying my dishes to the kitchen.

Kris follows me. As I set the dirty plates and glasses in the sink, we can hear Grandma slowly walking through the dining room and living room, then climbing the stairs. She always leans forward, as if for momentum, gripping the railing. Her hand slides up in jerks as her foot reaches the next step. Stairs are a long process for her.

I fill the metal dishpan with soapy water. Kris leans against the counter beside me.

"I wonder," I say, pushing the dishrag into a glass, "how Grandma gets all her dishes washed when she's here alone. I mean, I've done the dishes after every meal since I got here. Grandma always seems so tired after dinner, and I wonder if she just lets them stack up until there aren't any clean plates."

Kris nods as he dries the glass. "My mom comes over and helps clean sometimes."

"I know that my mom has worried about her for years, even before Grandpa died. She didn't like the two of them living alone here, taking care of themselves, with Grandpa sick, and now she thinks Grandma shouldn't stay here. She tells her the house is too big and she's not so young anymore."

Kris smiles. "And your grandmother tells her she's just fine."

"That's right."

"She must be lonely, though."

"God, you'd think so. I mean, it's probably okay for some people to live alone, but after being married for fifty years or so . . . I remember after Grandpa was taken to the hospital that last time, and we were on the phone and Mom was making arrangements to drive out here, Grandma said that she was going to sleep on the couch, because she'd never slept alone in their bed. She just couldn't face that empty bed."

We finish the dishes in silence. I rinse the dishpan while Kris hangs up the towel, and when I turn from the sink he's right there, his body barely an inch from mine.

"I haven't kissed you yet," he whispers.

He holds me; his mouth comes close. At the last moment I jerk my head around. His hands tighten at my waist as he asks what's wrong.

I don't know what's wrong, except that we haven't been alone together since last Saturday night. And since that night I've remembered every day what it felt like when he touched and kissed my breast. Remembered and wanted it again; but remembered, too, Sam and that girl in Jeff's car, how out of control they were.

I twist to break free of him and say, "Let's watch some TV."

We sit together on the couch, which is awkward for watching television, since he has to lean around me to see the screen. He stays close to me, holding my hand, his shoulder brushing mine. Each touch tightens my stomach muscles; each touch makes me remember again. I'm not paying attention to the movie that's playing, but I notice when a man and a woman start kissing. The camera comes in close; we hear their heavy sighs. Kris's hand squeezes mine, then I feel his lips on my neck.

I jerk away. "Don't!"

He drops my hand and looks at me as though I've just announced I want to blow up the world. He starts to speak, stops, then asks if I want him to leave.

I look away, considering lying and deciding against it. "It's just," I say as softly as I can, "that I'm afraid . . . afraid that if you touch me, if we kiss, I'm going to want—"

He takes my hand again. "Want what?" I'm silent, staring at the floor, and he adds, "Want what we did Saturday night?"

I nod. "And more."

I feel his stillness, momentary yet electric. Then he says my name and touches my cheek. "Look at me."

Regretting my honesty, I lift my head. I can't meet his eyes. We sit motionless for a moment, then he leans forward to kiss me. A quick kiss, so quick I don't have time to pull back.

"Was that okay?" he asks.

I nod.

"Don't move," he says, and kisses my cheek, my temple, my ear, my neck.

He's not out of control. Nowhere near it. Each movement seems precise, as if he's concentrating on an experiment in chemistry. But I feel my breath quickening, feel my excitement rising, all from kisses on my face. I turn my head to catch his mouth with mine.

His arms swoop around me and he falls back on the couch, pulling me with him. I lie on top of him, mouth to mouth, hip to hip. As we kiss, I don't worry about technique, don't worry about the lights and television still on, don't worry about Grandma upstairs. I want more than his kisses, and sigh as his hands tug my T-shirt from my shorts. He pushes it up, pushes my bra up, working a hand between us to touch my breast.

My hips press down against his, instinct driving me: He pushes back, hips rising, hand at my back holding me tight to him. Then his hands are beneath my arms, urging me upward. I don't understand at first, then I feel his mouth seeking my breast. I shift; he finds it. I remind myself to listen for Grandma—she moves so slowly, we'd have plenty of time to pull ourselves back together if I hear her on the stairs. But then Kris moves me again, moves himself so we're lying side by side, his mouth still on my breast as his hand finds the front of my shorts.

I stop moving. He stops too, waiting, breathing hard, lips touching my nipple. I don't think, I can't think. Something rigid—fear, common sense—loosens inside me, and I nudge my hips against his hand. He hesitates, then slips his hand between the shorts and my skin, caressing my stomach, down to the top of my underwear. He stops; his hand can't go any farther. He whispers my name, then pulls his hand back out to unfasten the shorts.

Again, I don't move. If I move, I'll think. If I think, I'll stop him.

His hand is back, slipping all the way down my body, no hesitation this time. My eyes squeeze shut, then he's touching me. He waits, then slides his finger along me, exploring. My thigh muscles tense, as though to force his hand away, but I do not stop him. Not until he whispers, "You're so wet."

His voice, the words, have the same effect as hearing Grandma's step on the stairs. Embarrassed, anxious, afraid, I pull back so suddenly, I roll off the couch onto the floor.

"Ginnie!" He leans over the edge. "Are you all right?"

I want to laugh at his alarm, but the tingling where he touched me holds my attention. Such a light, brief touch, yet so powerful. Too powerful. I scramble to my feet, turning away as I tug down my bra and T-shirt, then re-fasten my shorts.

When I turn around, he's standing, looking worried, maybe afraid, too, as he asks if I'm okay.

I nod.

He tries to hold me, but I step back.

"You want me to go?"

I nod once more.

He reaches out to touch my shoulder, then leaves.

TWENTY-FOUR

nsomnia kept me up until after one, yet I can't manage to sleep late the next morning. Stunningly bright, the sun seems to shine through crystal, its light glinting off the white garage, the slate stepping-stones, each blade of grass. Unsmudged by heat, the sky is clear and deep; all of the trees and bushes and flowers gleam as though last night's torrent polished them to their finest gloss. The air flows sweet and soft, even cool, and I wear jeans instead of shorts down to breakfast.

After gulping down my cereal and a blueberry muffin, I race back upstairs to call Mom. As I punch out the number, I rehearse what I'll say. I just want to ask her—not that anything's happened to me—what it means when two people make love. Tell her something I read in a book seemed silly and I was wondering . . .

The phone rings and rings. I count twelve of them and hang up.

"Dammit," I whisper. Where is she? At work? Oh God, is she at work? Does she work the whole day?

I trudge down the stairs and head for the back door. Grandma asks if something is wrong, if Kris and I had a fight. A fight I could handle. I tell her I'm okay.

She's speaking again as I head out the door, but I don't stay. Though I want to walk straight down the driveway and across the street to his house, I force myself to go into the garage, take down the gardening tools, and put on that ridiculous, battered straw hat. I walk down to the garden, then drop onto one of the stone steps and stare blindly at the flowers.

I spend the day alone, working in the garden all morning, pulling weeds and cutting off dead blossoms, then picking a bouquet for the dining room. After lunch I go back to the garden with a book I bought a couple of days ago, a romance that takes place in twelfth-century Britain. It's good, and I easily lose myself in it, half falling in love with the hero, a young, impetuous, high-spirited man with flaming red hair. I can even see myself as the heroine, tall and thin and plain, with brown hair that brightens in the light.

A little after five, Grandma starts making a chef's salad for dinner, and I call Mom again. Still not home.

I wait until after the dishes are done and we've watched the national news before trying her again. Sitting cross-legged on my bed, the phone tight against my ear, I carefully dial. She answers on the second ring.

We chat for a while about the weather, her day at work, then she asks what I've been up to.

"I've . . . uh, I've been reading a lot." I trace the pattern on my bedspread with my finger. "Like this book I was reading today. It takes place in the twelfth century, in Britain, and it's about this woman who's forced to marry this man, a lord, because her family thinks he . . . uh, debauched her when he was drunk. He didn't, and on their wedding night he tells her that he won't touch her until she wants him to."

"Very understanding of him," my mother says.

"Well, eventually she falls in love with him and they . . . make love."

"Uh-huh."

"And it just got me thinking. . . . Of course, they're married, so it's okay they make love, but once they do, they're sort of stuck with each other, aren't they?"

"That's not the most romantic way of putting it, but that's generally the idea."

"But what if they made love and she didn't want to stay with him?"

Mom pauses, as if trying to decipher my real question, then says, "I don't know about the twelfth century, but nowadays she can just leave, even if they're married. But why would she want to?"

"Well . . . maybe she's not ready for marriage. Ready to stay in one place."

Longer pause from Mom this time, then she asks, "Are we talking about fictional characters, or someone I know?"

I don't answer, not sure how honest to be. It's not like I

can tell her what happened on the sofa last night, tell her how Kris made me feel and how much those feelings disturbed me. But why else did I want to talk to her so badly, if not to be honest?

"We're not talking about me," I answer at last. "Not really. I just was wondering what would happen . . . That is, if once you and a guy are lovers, if it's okay to leave. Or if you should stay. I mean, what sort of commitment have you made?"

"That's a bit open-ended, Ginnie. Any commitment between two people is unique to them. And, to my way of thinking, if there's no emotional commitment before the lovemaking, then the lovemaking doesn't mean much. Not in terms of commitment. Not in terms of staying."

"Oh." My next question is, How do you know if there's an emotional commitment? But I think the answer is, If you have to ask, there isn't one. And, on the flip side, if you think making love with someone commits you to him, then a commitment has probably already been made. No wonder I was so scared last night.

"Ginnie? You okay?"

"Yeah, I'm okay. It's just that a lot of things have been thrown at me this summer, and I'm trying to figure some of them out.

"There's this girl here, you see. Diane. I told you about her. Anyhow, she thinks it's okay to have sex with any guy. Well, that's what she says, and I'm not sure she really believes it. But she doesn't think it means anything, that it's just for fun."

"And you don't think it is?"

"Well, really, Mom, I wouldn't exactly know."

216

She laughs. "Okay. Point taken. I'm not sure what to tell you, Ginnie, except that sex is one of our society's more touchy issues. Many people seem to be afraid of it. They don't like to talk about it, don't like to admit how important it is to all of us. But it's important in different ways to each of us, and it means something different at different times in our lives, with different lovers. Your friend may say it's fun now, but in a few years she might fall head over heels in love and it won't be 'just for fun.' It will be the most special thing in her life. And there may be another girl who says she's going to wait for Mr. Right, but she meets a man who's definitely Mr. Wrong but who is so attractive, she can't resist him. And she learns that lovemaking can be fun and not necessarily a lifetime commitment." She pauses, then asks, "Is this making sense?"

"Sort of." I spend a few moments picturing Diane "head over heels in love" and myself panting after a gorgeous Mr. Wrong. Neither picture is believable. But I think Mom's saying what I've always figured. If you know it's right, then do it. If you can't handle the consequences, then don't. And the consequences of making love with Kris would be love itself. Maybe I love him already, but actual lovemaking would make the love real, undeniable. It would have to be dealt with every day, and I don't want to do that. Maybe next year, or during college, or after college, when I'm free to choose where I live, which direction I want to go, but not now.

"It does make sense, Mom. I mean, in the abstract. This is all theory yet for me."

"Well, when you move from theory into experimentation, be careful. On the practical side, there's the risk of pregnancy and the risk of disease, especially AIDS, so make sure you're protected. And from an emotional viewpoint, we all make mistakes, we all meet the wrong guy at some point and make fools of ourselves. Just don't . . . don't give more than you can."

Sentimentality is creeping into her voice. Time to end this. "I gotta go, Mom. I don't want to run up Grandma's phone bill."

"Before you go, Ginnie. Are you sure you're okay? I mean, this isn't about Denny breaking up with you, is it?"

Denny? He hadn't even crossed my mind. "No, Mom, Denny's history. And he didn't hurt me that badly. I can handle it."

She laughs a little. "Do you remember what you said to me last spring when you had a crush on that basketball player?"

I groan. "You mean Bill? No, what did I say?"

"When I asked you how it was going with him, you told me he was really hooked on his girlfriend, and that he wasn't ever going to be anything but a friend to you. Then I asked if you were all right, and you said, 'I'm fine, Mom. I'm tough.'" She laughs again, but not in a hurtful way. "You looked so sad and mournful, but you were going to tough your way through it." Her voice deepens with seriousness again. "You are tough. You're going to be okay, even when things are at their worst."

"Are you tough, Mom?"

"I'm getting there, Ginnie. I'm getting there."

I'm on the phone with Diane the next morning, staring out the living-room window at Kris's house, when his front door opens and he steps onto the porch. He heads straight across the street. I turn away, arm across my middle, trying to focus on Diane again.

"He finally kissed me last night," she's saying, continuing the long description of her latest date with Steve, "and, you know, it was pretty nice. But he also told me his girlfriend's coming back next week, and he can't just say to her as soon as she gets off the plane that he's dating Diane LaSalle. So it just end right here."

"I'm sorry, Diane."

"It's okay." She doesn't sound okay, though. "I mean, I never expected anything much out of this. He's really not my type."

"But still, if you like the guy . . ." I hear footsteps on the porch. "I gotta go, Diane. Kris is here."

"Speaking of liking a guy," she says.

Kris knocks on the door and I almost run across the room, slipping on the small Oriental rug in front of the door. I steady myself on the bookcases as I say hi. He smiles back, looking uncertain of his welcome, and I ask if he wants to go out back. Grandma is upstairs, and I really don't want her eavesdropping. He says sure, and we troop down to the garden.

We sit side by side on the bottom step, and I stare at the flowerless stems of the day lilies. Neither of us speaks for a minute, then he asks if I'm mad at him.

I turn my head to stare at him. "Mad at you? No. Is that what you thought when I asked you to go?"

He nods, looking down at the ground. "What we did . . . I knew it was going too fast for you."

"But not you?"

"I don't know. I wasn't thinking. I only knew I wanted to touch you. I wanted . . ."

"To make love?"

He lifts his head, smiling briefly. "Not on your grandmother's couch. And not . . . I don't know what I wanted."

I think I do. He wanted that connection, that bond between us. Not just sex, but commitment. "Kris, I can't."

"I know," he says swiftly, but I touch his hand to quiet him.

"Not can't make love, but can't . . . stay."

He leans back, frowning. "What do you mean?"

"I'm going to leave in a few days." I didn't know I would until I said the words, but I know it's right. Still, I hate to see the hurt in his eyes. "I'm sorry, but I have to."

He's so motionless, he doesn't seem to breathe. Then he takes my hand. "If you have to, I can't come with you." He looks out across the garden. "I asked my parents and they said no. They don't think it would be a good idea. And they don't want to have to pay for me to fly home."

"I'm sorry."

He squeezes my hand. "I am too. When . . . Will you come back sometime?"

I nod. "Maybe in October. Mom and I came over Columbus Day weekend last year. Definitely for Thanksgiving. And we can write."

"Yes, but . . ." He looks straight at me. "I'm going to miss you."

"Me too." Bearing down on the swelling ache inside me, I smile brightly. "But we've got a date for next summer. You're going to go to Italy with me."

He grins. "That's right. And I'll hold you to that."

His grin collapses. He hugs me fiercely. "You're the first girl," he whispers, "who ever liked me."

I hide my face in his neck. "I like you a lot. Do you want to go out tonight?"

"Every night until you leave." He moves back to see my face. "You're not going to leave tomorrow, are you?"

"No. Monday. Less traffic then."

"So you'll want to spend Sunday night with your grandmother."

"Maybe you could come for dinner. Sort of a going-away."

He nods, sobered again, and I kiss him. Since we now have only three days, my caution eases. A summer of separations magnifies love's value; I let it warm me. It can't hurt me now, and it might make the parting easier.

"I think I'm falling in love with you," I whisper.

He runs a shaking hand over my hair. "I'm falling in love with you, too."

T W E N T Y - F I V E

I tell Grandma during dinner that I'll be leaving.

"Oh!" She puts down her fork and looks mournfully at me. "I was hoping this would never end." She laughs. "But of course it has to. Of course you have to go home. Your mother needs you."

My eyes narrow suspiciously. "What do you mean, my mother needs me?"

"She does. This is a very hard time for her, Ginnie. You're old enough now to help her through this, help her find her way back to your father. Part of being a grown-up is taking responsibility."

I scowl at my cold macaroni salad. I'm not going home to take care of my mother. Her relationship with Dad is her problem. My relationships with the two of them, as separate people, not a single entity, is my problem. Unless

Mom drags me into whatever anger and disappointment she's feeling for Dad.

I stab a chunk of ham. I won't let that happen. If she's angry at him, I won't be angry. I won't defend him to her, or feed any fires. I'll be aloof. A referee.

I like that image, and concentrate on it as Grandma's voice washes over me.

Her assertion that my parents would never separate for good is interrupted by the phone. I hastily wipe my mouth and rush into the living room to answer it.

"Hi, Ginnie. It's Tom."

"Tom!" I drop onto the sofa in surprise. "Where are you?"

"I'm in Philadelphia." His dry tone implies that being in Philadelphia ain't what it used to be.

"When'd you get back?" I ask.

"Late last night. I drove straight down from Maine with a friend. Quite a shock to go from six weeks in the backwoods of Maine to this."

Not certain if "this" refers to our Philadelphia suburb or Mom and Dad, I ask hesitantly, "Did you . . . did Mom write you?"

He laughs, and I never realized before how much his laugh is like Grandma's. The same "I don't know what to say so I'll laugh as if everything is under control" quality. "She wrote me," he says, "but I think she left out a few details."

"Is she there now?"

"No. She went out to dinner with a friend."

"Oh."

"What happened, Ginnie?" His voice is even, rational.

No horror or shock, but maybe he's already gotten over that. Then again, Tom never dwells on what might have been. He takes what's handed to him and deals with it.

I almost say I don't know what happened, that no one ever told me. But then I wonder what he knew. He's hardly been home for years, so did he realize, even subconsciously, what was happening? Being older and less dependent on them, he could have seen more clearly what all the little things meant. Dad's evening job, Mom's restlessness, the Saturday nights when they didn't go out anymore, their not liking each other's friends.

"Don't *you* know what happened?" I ask him.

"I haven't been here, Ginnie. How would I know?"

"Well, I guess it's been going on for a while, maybe even before you left for college. I thought maybe you would have figured things out. That that's why you don't come home anymore."

"I come home. I knew things weren't great between them, but for Dad to actually move out . . . Is there another woman?"

I grab my side as though he's punched me. That question has lurked in my mind, even before Diane asked me, yet I haven't dared to confront it. "I don't know," I say crossly, as if he's asked me to explain why the universe was created. "I didn't think to ask him."

"What about Mom?"

"Tom! I don't know! I haven't been home all summer either, you know."

"Hey, Ginnie. Calm down."

Grandma's leaning far across the table to see me, eyes

wide with curiosity. I drop my head down, my hair covering my face.

"I'm calm. I'm coming home on Monday."

"You flying?"

"No, driving. Grandma's giving me Grandpa's car."

"You're kidding! That's great. Grandpa's car. That's great."

"Yeah. And you can't take it to college with you."

"Wouldn't think of it. You'll have fun when you pull that monster into the parking lot at school."

"That's what I figured."

We've gotten off the subject, and I'm not about to get us back onto it.

"So you're driving by yourself, huh?"

"Sure am. Tell Mom, would you? She told me last Saturday that either I could drive back myself or she'd fly out here and we'd drive back together. I've decided to do it myself."

"I think you're ready for it." He pauses. "So I guess we can talk when you get here."

That sounds ominous, real.

"I think it's important," he goes on, "that you and I stick together. We shouldn't let them use us, make us take sides against each other."

"They wouldn't do that," I say, ignoring the fact that I had thought that myself only a few minutes ago.

"I'm not saying they would," he answers patiently. "But in case they try, we have to say no. Our loyalties should be to each other first."

"Each other?" I whisper. How can I so completely

detach myself from my parents? Yet isn't that what I've been saying all summer I want to do?

"It'll be all right, Ginnie. We'll talk when you get home. Maybe we can go out for breakfast or lunch on Tuesday. Do you know the route to take to get here?"

"Yeah, the Pennsylvania Turnpike." I don't mean to be sarcastic, but his words have frightened me.

He ignores the sarcasm anyway. "I mean, do you know how to get on and off the Turnpike?"

"I know where to go when I get off, but I don't know how to go from here. I'm going to call Dad tonight and ask him to give me the directions. He doesn't know when I'm coming yet."

"Okay. So I'll see you Monday. Let me talk to Grandma now."

I stand, picking up the phone. "Tom wants to talk to you, Grandma."

"Don't bring the phone to the dinner table," she scolds, as I start for the dining room.

She meets me halfway and carries the phone back to her chair. She waits to speak until she's comfortably settled, phone in her lap, feet just on the edge of the needlepoint-covered footstool, head high.

"Hello, Tom. How *are* you?"

I carry my glass into the kitchen to get more milk, then stay there, staring out the big window over the backyard. I catch Grandma's laugh and a few of her words—thrilling, delightful, hot. I'm trying not to listen, trying not to do anything but look out, beyond the fresh parsley and mint flourishing in a window box to the bushes and trees that edge the lawn and hide the neighbors' yards.

226

"Oh, it's so good to hear your voice," Grandma says. "Call again soon. 'Bye."

Before she has even hung up I'm back in the living room. "I'm going to call Dad."

She nods and returns to the dining room as I sit back down on the couch. Dad's number is written on a pad thrown together with innumerable scraps of paper on the table beside me. The phone rings without an answer. Eventually I hang up.

"He probably just went out for dinner," Grandma says as I return to the table. "He'll be in later."

"I'm going out with Kris in a little bit." I stare at the macaroni salad left on my plate. My stomach rolls threateningly and I push the plate away. "I'm sorry, Grandma. I'm not hungry anymore."

"Tom sounded wonderful. He said he had a good summer." She shifts in that familiar useless attempt to straighten her back. "He didn't write very often."

"He doesn't have the chance to send that many letters, Grandma. They're only at the base camp for a few days throughout the whole six weeks."

She clicks her tongue, obviously not impressed with my reasoning. "None of you write very often," she says, looking at the portrait of that unknown ancestor. "I suppose your mother didn't impress that upon you well enough. Why, when she was younger, she used to write to your grandfather and me every week. Every week. But I suppose she's too busy now with her job and her new friends, and soon you will be, too, when you go off to college and start having all sorts of new adventures."

"Grandma . . ." The glimmer of pain in her eyes

227

accuses me, even though the tilt of her head denies any pain. She's tough, though, I think. Like Mom and me. I vow to write her every week when I get home.

When she says nothing more, I pick up my plate and empty milk glass and carry them to the kitchen. She doesn't move as I clear her dishes too. I quickly wash them, then cover the bowl of salad and put it in the refrigerator. Someone knocks at the door as I finish wiping off the counters.

"Kris is here," Grandma calls.

I hurry past her to the living room. She still hasn't moved.

"I'm just about ready," I say to Kris, opening the door.

I run up the stairs as Grandma greets him. I can't hear what he says, but I hear her tinkling laugh.

I call Dad a little after nine Saturday morning. The phone rings five times before it's answered. There's a pause, then he mumbles, "Hello?"

"Dad? Did I wake you up?"

"Oh, Ginnie." He groans. "I'm sorry, dear. I slept later than I thought."

"Do you want me to call you back?"

"No, no. I'll wake up in a minute."

"I'm coming home on Monday."

"Good." The enthusiasm he forces into his groggy voice is pretty sad. "Is your friend coming with you?"

"No, he can't."

"That's too bad."

"I talked to Tom yesterday," I go on. "Have you seen him?"

"No. I'll see him today." He laughs. His attempt at tossing off unpleasant thoughts with a laugh is less successful than Grandma's. "I hope he's not too rough on me. Your brother can be pretty stern."

Conflicting loyalties tug within me. Just like Tom said they would. "Well, you know, Dad, someone could have told him. It must have been a shock for him to come home and find out."

"Your mother said she would write him."

Anger is brewing. My muscles tighten with the fear of confrontation. We're not a family that confronts. We'll have to learn.

"I need directions, Dad. I don't know how to get to the Turnpike from here."

"All right. Go down to Beverly Road and head north. Then—"

"Wait! How do I get there? Which way is north?"

"It's the way we always go."

"No, it's the way you always go. Mom goes a different way."

He pauses to take a deep breath and let it out, then starts over. "Go up Spruce Road and take the first left. Follow that down to the traffic light, about a mile, and go right. Then—"

He stops. "No. It's the quickest way, but I guess her way is easier. Go down Spruce and take a right."

Turn by turn, he describes precisely the way to the Turnpike. He warns me where the intersections are tricky, where a merge onto one of the city's freeways has to be made at fifty miles an hour, or I'll be stranded. Dad's always good at details.

When he's done, he tells me that if I get lost to stop and call him collect at his office. And not to panic.

"I won't," I promise.

As soon as I hang up I want to call him again, tell him I'm not coming back. I don't want to see them, deal with them, the empty house, the explanations and excuses. Even to face my friends at school, their questions, their sympathy. And Denny. Oh God, what will he say to me?

The drive has lost its sheen too. Instead of seeing the road rising and dropping, curving through the mountains with Grandma Moses views of farms below, I see the tunnels. The narrow tunnels blasted with the noise and fumes of speeding diesel trucks. I'm not going back.

All of my muscles tighten again. I clutch my arms so hard, I can feel the bones beneath the skin. Staring blindly at the old upright piano, pictures of my family on top, I tell myself I can change my mind. I still have to go, but Mom can fly out like she said she would. Yet if I give in, if I don't drive alone, I'll have failed.

I remember facing the concrete floor in our basement one night, deciding, when no one was home, to teach myself how to do cartwheels. I did.

I have to face this too. All of it.

TWENTY-SIX

The weather's perfect for one last day at the pool. The sky, hazy with heat, is dotted with cotton-candy clouds; a light breeze counters the piercing rays of sun. Kris and I walk slowly, arms around each other, knowing this is the last time. We don't talk much, except that he tells me he wants to take me out to dinner that night. His dad said he could drive his car.

Diane and her friends are there. I point Kris to the opposite side of the pool from them.

Smoothing out my towel, I notice Barbara is sitting apart from her boyfriend, her back to him as she talks to another guy. Larry, Diane's ex, is there, and he reaches out to gently prod her arm. She scowls and pushes his hand away, but she doesn't turn from him.

Kris has spread his towel out. Instead of lying down and reading like he always does, he sits beside me, looking around.

"I wonder if this is exciting for anyone," he says abruptly.

"What do you mean?"

"It's the big thing for high-school kids to do, hang out at the pool all summer. It always sounds . . ." He shrugs. "Exciting. But it's just the same thing every day."

"My dad says that when you get right down to it, life's pretty boring. It is the same thing every day."

"I don't want my life to be boring."

I drape my arms over my drawn-up knees and tilt my head back, squinting at the sun. "I don't either. I want . . . I don't know. I want people to know who I am. I want . . . " I drop my head back down and look at him. "I want girls to see me and wish they were me. Does that make any sense?"

He nods.

"What do you want?"

"I don't know. I just don't want to be bored. I don't want to live the kind of life my parents have, the same routine day in and day out. Like your father said." He gestures to the group across the pool. "I bet they'll lead boring lives. They'll do the same thing their parents do, even if they rebel against them now. They don't have the imagination to do anything different."

"That's not fair," I say, though I wonder if he's right. "Anyone can change their life."

He shakes his head. "I don't think so."

We sit in silence. Diane is laughing at Larry, swatting

his hands away as he tries to grab her. Barbara's standing up now, hands on her hips, posing for that guy. Michelle posed like that last summer, standing over Denny as he lay on the lounge chair with his bandaged leg. It's the same little game, the one I was never very good at. Maybe, I think, that's okay.

I lie down and close my eyes. I don't want to read, but simply take in all the sounds around me so I can remember this. Kris lies down, too, and holds my hand.

My new blue-and-white dress does make me feel older, even pretty. As I run down the stairs, I wonder if this time Grandma will notice my lack of a bra. She doesn't mention it.

"Kris should be very proud to escort you this evening," she says.

With effort, I accept the compliment, not turning it aside with a joke. "Thank you."

I perch on the edge of Grandpa's chair, squelching the sudden urge to go to the bathroom. I just went. Twice. After checking my pockets again for tissues and money, I examine my nails. I considered painting them with Mom's red polish—I brought it from Philadelphia—but it reminded me too much of Diane. Instead, I put it on my toenails. I lift my legs, holding my feet up so I can admire the bright color.

For the first time, Kris is late. I fidget in the big armchair, trying not to stare out the door, even though it's directly in front of me. Studying the buttons on my dress, I wonder if I can get away with unfastening the bottom two. Or would that be too daring? I'm considering how much of my leg would be revealed when he knocks on the door. I jump.

"Hi," I exclaim too loudly. "I'm ready. 'Bye, Grandma."

"Have a nice time, you two," she calls after us.

Kris didn't bother to bring the car over, so we walk back across the street and down his driveway. His father's car is a dark-blue Ford, smaller than Grandpa's. He opens my door for me, then closes it when I'm settled. As he slides behind the wheel and starts the engine, I wonder about moving over. I'm too nervous, though, and stay where I am.

The restaurant he's chosen is much nicer than the Country Squire. A waitress tells us the specials for the night and asks if we'd like anything to drink. Kris orders a soda. I ask for water.

As we study the menus, I reach under the table and undo those two bottom buttons. Then I cross my legs and glance down. Oh Christ. The skirt falls away to reveal half my thigh. I can't get the higher button refastened with one hand, and Kris keeps glancing at me as if he knows I'm up to something. I leave the buttons alone and read the menu.

"Is Diane still going out with Steve?" he asks after we order.

"I don't think so." I chomp on some ice. "She told me the other day that his girlfriend is coming back from Europe soon."

"You shouldn't chew ice, Ginnie. It cracks the enamel on your teeth. Do you think she really likes Steve?"

I shrug, letting the ice melt in my mouth. "I think so,

234

but she was putting on her tough-girl act, you know, pretending she didn't care."

"If I see them together in school, I'll let you know."

"Good."

The mention of school sombers us. "What courses are you taking this year?" Kris asks.

"Mostly English. I've already fulfilled the math and science requirements. I could take calculus or chemistry, but I really don't want to. Actually, I don't even need that many more credits overall. I could probably graduate after the first semester."

"Why don't you? Why don't you take the courses you need first semester and leave?"

"Because . . ."

"Both Nicole and Eli did that."

"What would I do instead?"

He shrugs. "Work? You could start earning money for college."

I think about it, intrigued. Maybe Kris is right. All it takes is a little imagination to make our lives different.

After dinner he drives to the same neighborhood, parks in the same spot. He reaches to turn off the radio, but I stop him.

"Can we listen to it for a while?"

"It wears down the battery."

"Just for a couple of minutes."

"Okay."

He shuts off the engine, and we listen to an ad for acne cream.

"So this is it," I say stupidly.

He nods, his face shadowed. "This is the best summer I've ever had."

I laugh shortly. "I can't really say the same, but you were certainly the best part of it."

I slide my left leg up to lie bent on the seat, forgetting about those damn buttons. Kris's gaze fastens on my legs, and I look down. The inside of my thigh is exposed, dark against the light fabric. I start to jerk the skirt closed, but his hand is already there, his fingers lightly stroking my skin.

He doesn't say anything, just keeps trailing his fingers back and forth, never wandering too high, yet not high enough. I don't realize I'm holding my breath until he looks at me. The yearning in his face, his eyes, tells me what he wants. I gasp in some air and frantically shake my head.

"No, Kris. I can't."

His whole palm lies against my thigh, warm and firm. If he moves that hand, slides it higher, I'll take the no back. If he kisses me just the right way, I'll say yes. We don't move, staring at each other, our breathing short, jerky.

He lifts his hand away and grips the wheel. "I really want to, Ginnie," he whispers, "but I don't think we should. Not with you leaving. It'll only make it harder."

I collapse back against the door, all muscles giving way at once. Though relieved he won't push me, I wonder if maybe that's what I want. I try to think of something to say. "That's a good song" is all I come up with.

Kris has gotten used to my love for rock and roll, and only sighs as he glances at the radio, cocking his head as if to hear better. "What is it?"

"'Bobby Jean' by Bruce Springsteen. The live version."

He frowns, obviously trying to make sense of the

sometimes mumbled words. "What's it about?"

"This girl he was best friends with, the only person who ever really understood him. But she just left one day without saying good-bye. So the song's his way of saying good-bye to her."

Kris eases across the seat and cups my face in his hands. "You wouldn't do that, go off without saying good-bye."

I shake my head. "I'm gonna miss you." It's probably the tenth time I've said that in two days.

"Me too. I wish you didn't have to go."

"I know. But we can write each other. I've promised myself I'm going to write Grandma once a week. I can write you at the same time." I pause. "Though I may want to write you more often than that."

"That's okay. We could even talk on the phone. Maybe once a month."

I nod. "I don't think Mom would mind."

"Ginnie . . . Are you going to be all right? I mean, do you think your parents will get back together?"

I hold on to his wrists, looking down. My left leg, still dangerously bare, presses against his. I like that we're this comfortable with each other. "I don't know if they'll get back together. I've been telling myself that it's not going to be too rough, but . . . I think it's going to be pretty bad."

His hands slide around my back. "But what you said that night when you had dinner at my place, that you're separate from them. It's true. You just have to adjust."

I nod against his shoulder. "I know. I've got to grow up. And I will. I want to. I just think this is going too fast."

He holds me and rocks me to U2's "With or Without You."

TWENTY-SEVEN

Sunday I pack. My two suitcases, the green overnight bag that Grandma gave me and Mom's boxy one from college, overflow with clothes. Fortunately, dozens of empty boxes teeter atop old, dusty furniture in Grandma's cluttered basement. I haul four upstairs and fill them. It doesn't take long. We run a couple of loads of laundry, then I quickly fold and pack the clothes, leaving out shorts, a shirt, and underwear for tomorrow.

Kris comes over in the afternoon and sits on my bed, watching morosely, picking through my books as I box them, then putting them back. We don't talk much.

Diane calls. I had called her the day before but she wasn't home, and now she says she's sorry she won't get to see me.

"We've got company coming for dinner," she explains. "They'll be here in a little while, so I can't go out. Maybe later tonight . . ."

"No," I say, sitting down beside Kris. "I have to go to bed early so I can get plenty of sleep."

"Yeah. That's wild, you driving the whole way to Philadelphia by yourself. Are you nervous?"

"Not really. It's just the tunnels that bother me."

"Oh man, yeah. Those things are scary. I always think that with just one little turn of the wheel, you'd go crashing into the wall."

"Thanks, Diane. I needed to hear that."

"Sorry."

"It looked like you and Larry were getting along okay at the pool the other day."

"I guess. He found out about me going out with Steve and that made him kind of crazy. Jealous, you know. I told him that he broke up with me and I could go out with whoever I wanted, and he got mad. He wants to go out with me this week, but I told him I'd give him an answer later."

I may not like Larry and I may think she's stupid to consider going out with him again, but at least she's got him under control. For now. "What about Steve?" I ask.

"I don't know. He called me yesterday from work. His girlfriend comes back on Wednesday, and he wants to see me sometime before then. Maybe we'll go out tomorrow night."

"He's a nice guy, Diane." Christ, I sound like Kris.

"Yeah. Maybe too nice. I don't know. Write me sometime, huh? And let me know if you're coming back. I guess you'll want to see Kris again."

"Yes. I might be back in October. Probably for Thanksgiving."

"That's great. Well, I gotta go help with dinner. Have a fun time driving back. Don't pick up any hitchhikers."

"No, I won't. Hey, Diane . . . I'm sorry we didn't spend more time together."

"Yeah, me too. My mom thinks you're a good influence on me."

I laugh. "Take care of yourself, Diane."

I hang up and Kris slides off the bed. "Did you get everything out of the closet?" he asks, opening the door.

"I think so."

Grandma's winter dresses hang inside, shrouded in dry-cleaner's plastic. Kris pokes among them, but none of my clothes are there. While I check under the bed, he opens the little drawer in the vanity. He pushes aside the handkerchiefs, then sweeps his hand toward the back.

"Here's something."

He holds up a crushed pack of Kents, and I laugh as I take them from him. "I knew I had some around here someplace."

"I haven't seen you smoke for a while."

"I know. I ran out last week and just never felt like buying more. I usually only smoke around other people who smoke, you know."

"Or when I say something that upsets you."

I glance at him, but he's peering into the drawer again. "Like you said, I haven't smoked for a while."

He tossed me a small smile over his shoulder, then straightens. "Who's this?" he asks, showing me a wallet-sized black-and-white photograph.

"My mother. She was about ten and the flower girl at someone's wedding."

He studies the girl in the picture, her curled hair covered by a frilly bonnet, her long dress so stiff and starched, it probably stood upright even when she wasn't in it. "She doesn't look at all like you," he says. "Except the eyes. You have her eyes. And they're not your grandmother's eyes."

"No. I don't look like her or Grandma."

He puts the picture back. "I like the way you look."

"Even if I'm too skinny and have a big nose?"

"You don't have a big nose."

I cross my eyes to look at it. "Yes, I do."

"And you're not too skinny."

He's staring right at my breasts when he says that, and I laugh and playfully shove him. He laughs too. It's a perfect moment I won't ever forget.

Grandma makes my favorite meal for dinner—fried chicken, rice cooked with chicken broth, and fresh green beans. We even light candles and turn off the overhead light.

We don't speak for a few minutes, which is all right with me. No one makes chicken as good as my grandmother's, and I'm content to concentrate on it.

"You know, Ginnie," she says eventually, "I really have enjoyed having you here. You've become a delightful young woman."

I wipe my mouth. "I've enjoyed being here, Grandma. Really."

"It's good you made friends. Will you and Kris be writing each other?"

"Yes. And I'll write you, too."

She smiles. "Thank you, dear." She eats a forkful of rice, then sits back and sighs. "It's hard to believe another summer is nearly gone. Your grandfather loved summertime. The long evenings, the quiet, the slower pace . . ."

"The baseball games."

She laughs merrily. "Oh, yes, the baseball games. It's as I said when you first got here, Ginnie. Someday you'll find a man to share all those things with, and you'll understand how precious it is."

I cut off a slice of chicken.

"It may not be the first man you love," she goes on, "but when you find the right man, you'll know. And if you work hard, it'll last forever."

I resent the implication that my parents' failure is solely their fault, that there wasn't some outside force shoving them apart. But I don't want to talk about my parents. Tomorrow is soon enough.

"What if I fall in love with the wrong man?" I ask. "What if he's the one I want?"

Will she now, since I'm leaving, tell me the last bit about Charles, how it felt to love him and know she couldn't have him? I want to know if it was hard for her, what price she paid for the love.

"You have to give him up," she answers, delicately spearing a green bean. "That's all. You just have to give him up."

She won't tell. She'll leave me thinking it's easy not to choose the wrong man, easy to deny the love. And maybe

242

after all this time, giving up Charles was easy compared to everything else, to keeping the right man for fifty years, and then losing him.

We clean the kitchen, then I go upstairs to check once more that I've packed up everything. Kris calls, but we don't talk for long. Tears are multiplying inside me, and I don't want to let them loose until tomorrow. He tells me he'll come over at eight to say good-bye.

Back downstairs I dish out the ice cream. Vanilla with chocolate sauce for me; vanilla in a glass of ginger ale for her. We sit outside in the dark and listen to the crickets.

"Summer is ending," I say. "I read in a book once that crickets start chirping about six weeks before summer ends."

"That's right," Grandma says.

"Do you really want to stay here alone?"

She rests her glass in her lap. "It's been so nice having you here, Ginnie, I'm beginning to wonder. But I don't know how I could leave the house where I lived with your grandfather. It would be like losing him again."

I nod and eat my ice cream. After all that has happened, we seem to have said everything we can. Finishing our dessert, we go inside. She slowly climbs the stairs to take her bath, and I sit in the dark living room, listening to the sounds of the night, hoping I will always remember this.

T W E N T Y - E I G H T

I don't sleep well. I wake up about every two hours, thinking it must be time to get up, and groaning when my clock reads one, or three, or five. I asked Grandma to come get me at seven, but I'm wide awake at six and just get up. I hope I won't fall asleep at the wheel.

After a bath, I shiver as I put on my shorts and sleeveless shirt. The morning air is cool once more, but I know I'll be thankful for the shorts in a few hours.

Grandma is stirring in her bedroom as I tiptoe past. Downstairs it is quiet, the sun barely creeping in through the windows, the rooms in dismal dimness. I turn on the light in the kitchen, and the radio.

After my tea is ready I step out onto the back porch. It's quiet out there, too, except for the birds. A bus throttles its way up the hill, but I've grown so used to them, I scarcely notice. Mug in hand, I step down onto the grass. It's wet and cold against my bare feet, and I take giant steps along the slate stones that lead to the garden.

Hidden down there, I take the battered pack of Kents from my pocket and light one. For old time's sake, I tell myself, blowing out the match. But my first swallow of smoke sears along those little cilia. I cough, surprised at how easy it was to get out of the habit of smoking.

The second puff goes down more smoothly. I sit in contentment, not worrying about the time or the long drive ahead, or what I'll find in Philadelphia. I stop everything to just that moment, the hard stone I'm sitting on, the cool, lush grass, the soft air, the flash of blue as a jay swoops past. Somewhere, I decide, I'll find this again. I want to have a garden and early-morning silence. It's a goal of sorts. I carefully grind out my cigarette.

By the time I have loaded the two suitcases and the boxes of books and tapes and clothes into the trunk of the car, Grandma is cooking breakfast. Always a big breakfast before a trip. Scrambled eggs and sausage and coffee cake.

Except for putting my sneakers on, I'm ready when Kris arrives at eight. His whole body droops, his hands knocking nervously against his thighs. He was never one to hide anything, and his sadness is like match, sparking mine. This is the one thing I didn't want to do.

"So," he says, "you ready?"

I nod.

"Scared?"

"A little. It is a long way." I smile. "But the car's got a radio, so the music will help me along."

245

He looks down, running a foot across the living-room carpet, against the nap. He leaves a dark trail, then rubs it out. I drop down onto the couch and shove one foot into a sneaker.

He shuffles closer and stands over me. "Will you write me as soon as you get back?"

"Sure. Tonight. I'll mail it tomorrow and you should get it by Friday."

"Good. I'll write back right away."

Both sneakers are on and tied, and I stand up. We're so close, I imagine I can feel his warmth, can feel his chest swell with each breath. I take a tiny step nearer and his arms wrap around me. We hold on to each other, our hearts beating together. Hearing a noise, I peek over his shoulder. Grandma is standing in the arch between the living room and dining room. She watches us for just a moment, then turns back to the kitchen.

I want to stay in Kris's arms, but seeing Grandma has made me nervous. Awkwardly, I pull away, but he stops me with a kiss. It's a quick one; we're both uneasy with Grandma nearby and the packed car in the driveway. He releases me and I turn away.

Kris follows me out to the kitchen, where Grandma is waiting at the back door, unforgettable in her new blue jumper over a white blouse with full sleeves and ruffles at the neck and cuffs. My throat closes with pain. She looks so *familiar*, her hands flat against her hips, as if she's bracing herself; her head tilted back, for everyone is taller than she; the skin of her face as soft and finely lined as old, crumpled tissue paper.

I love her, I think, and suddenly hug her. She holds my

arms, her crooked fingers strong. Her body is firm and solid, and seems sturdier than mine.

"Thank you," she whispers, and goes up on tiptoe to kiss my cheek. "You drive safely."

Casting a quick look at Kris, I push out through the door. The key's in the ignition, and I turn it with a sharp jerk. The car rumbles and starts. I force myself to wait for the idle to kick down. From the corner of my eye I see them waiting at the open door; then Grandma touches Kris's arm. They move back and the door closes. They'll watch me go by from the front.

The engine smoothes out. I take a deep breath and push the reverse button. The car slides into gear and I barely need to depress the accelerator to get it moving. I pass the wide front porch. Grandma is at the door. In the rearview mirror I can see Kris at the end of the driveway, checking for traffic. He waves to me that it's all clear.

I back onto the street, turning the wheel hard to the right so I'm facing down the hill. The car drifts to the curb, and I stop. Kris walks around to my open window. He starts to speak, then ducks his head inside and kisses me. Not a quick, embarrassed kiss this time, but a kiss to savor all the way home. He steps back. His eyes shine silver with tears.

I nod as if he has said something and put the car in drive. Then I stop again, set the emergency brake, and push myself up through the wide window opening.

"Grandma!" I call, waving to her over the roof of the car. "I love you."

Her voice clear and sweet, she sings back, "I love you too, Ginnie."

Satisfied, I slip back into the car and release the brake. I smile at Kris. "So long."

"So long."

He steps back and I gun the engine, racing down the hill.

By the time I'm on the Turnpike, I know I'll be fine. I drove awkwardly from the suburb into the city, through the short Fort Pitt Tunnel and along the long bridge over the Monongahela River, aware that all the other drivers knew where they were going, while I checked Dad's directions every quarter mile. The merge onto the expressway that runs south, down the Monongahela and past the silent, ugly steel mills that clutter its bank for more than a mile, was as bad as Dad warned me. At least nothing was worse, not even the quick trip through the Squirrel Hill Tunnel. But the faster I drove, keeping up with the traffic, the wider Grandpa's car grew, threatening to clip fenders on my left and right. I tried to stay in the right lane, only worrying then about the concrete abutment.

The Turnpike is simple after that, but I have four more tunnels to deal with. Traffic isn't heavy; just a lot of trucks. Dad taught me a few rules about them.

If you're going to drive with the trucks, keep up to their speed. If you're going downhill and one's coming behind you, get out of his way. They're a pain on the mountains, forever playing tag. You pass them on the way up, then they speed by you on the way down, doing eighty or so, foot off the brake. Free fall, I call it.

When I reach the first Turnpike tunnel—the Allegheny, about an hour beyond Pittsburgh—I stay in the right lane, fifty miles an hour, like I did with the Fort Pitt and Squirrel Hill. But even Grandpa's car isn't so wide that I bump against the shiny walls, and I sigh as the tunnel fades behind me.

I ease the car back up to fifty-five, conscientiously checking my rearview mirror. A red convertible is on my tail.

"You're gonna cause an accident, buddy," I mutter, even as the car whips out from behind me into the left lane.

It catches up to me in seconds, then lingers. I glance over. A young man, sunglasses on, blond hair wild in the wind, is driving. He grins at me and gestures with one hand, thumb up in an "okay" sign. His mouth moves but I can't hear what he says. It might have been "Great car." Then he passes and is quickly gone.

Slowly, I ease my grip on the wheel. My taut shoulders sag; my back rests against the seat back. I turn the radio on, but the mountains block the Pittsburgh stations. Fiddling with the dial, I find, as expected, only a country station. I'll know I'm halfway home when I can get some rock and roll out of Harrisburg.

The next tunnel's coming up. I switch on my lights, hesitate, then swing into the left lane, between two trucks, my foot heavy on the gas. The faster through it, the sooner done with it. We blast through the tunnel doing sixty-five, and as I burst into the sunlight, I laugh and let the car free fall down the mountain.